T0199218

OUTSIDE
THE RED-HEADED NEGRO

SADIYA RABIA

authorHOUSE®

AuthorHouse™
1663 Liberty Drive
Bloomington, IN 47403
www.authorhouse.com
Phone: 1 (800) 839-8640

Published by AuthorHouse   09/03/2015

ISBN: 978-1-5049-2827-4 (sc)
ISBN: 978-1-5049-2826-7 (e)

Library of Congress Control Number: 2015948646

Print information available on the last page.

Any people depicted in stock imagery provided by Thinkstock are models, and such images are being used for illustrative purposes only. Certain stock imagery © Thinkstock.

This book is printed on acid-free paper.

To Syed and Elizabeth

CONTENTS

Episode 1. The Redheaded Negro 1

Episode 2. Kicked Out of Heaven 46

Episode 3. A Guiding Light 82

Episode 4. Somebody Walked Over My Grave 124

Episode 5. Guilt Ridden 155

Episode 6. Behind Bars 194

THE REDHEADED NEGRO

She pulled up to her house.

The one—*Oh, God*—with its door open.

Lotte got out of the Kia Soul. Then reached into the back for the grocery bag.

She stood on the walkway staring at the front door, holding the grocery bag in the crook of one thin, frail arm and the house keys in her free hand. The interior of the house showed through the opening—the flowery walls and the carpeting. It froze Lotte on the walkway as she approached the doorstep and she had to think, Did I lock the door when I left?

She was old at seventy-eight, but she wasn't forgetful. She could remember fifty years of memories, good and bad. She had locked the door before leaving to go shopping. She always did, since the crimes in this neighborhood that were reported every month—robbery, even murder—got her living extra careful. She wouldn't leave her own front door carelessly open and inviting like that. Lotte said, "Oh my God," and ran into the house and shut the door.

There.

Good thing she came home in time. Otherwise someone would've broken in. Maybe someone had broken in. Then they might still be in the house. Let's see, Lotte thought, starting to search the house. There's nothing out of place, nothing taken.

She carried her shopping bag to the kitchen, walking through the hall and passing the living room doorway. Then she stopped. The living room was empty, but the TV was on. Lotte snapped the TV off.

An empty carton of prune juice sat on the kitchen counter next to three used glasses.

Lotte picked up the carton and shook it. She said, "They drank all my prune juice."

The plates and dishes were thoughtfully cleaned and placed on the blue plastic rack by the sink, almost dry now.

"And they washed the dishes," Lotte said, appalled. "I was going to do the dishes. That does it. I'm calling the police."

She raced into the living room, grabbed the phone and punched a number.

Someone on the line spoke up—a woman's voice.

"Yeah?"

Lotte said, "Get me the police."

"Ma'am, this is a phone *sex* hotline."

"Oh, goodness gracious—" Lotte stopped. "Say, you wouldn't happen to have the police there, would you?"

The woman said, "Not the kind you'd want." She paused and said, "Oh hey, while I got you—you sound old, you're experienced, so you'd know. How do you get rid of the gag reflex?"

Lotte said, "Stop sticking tools down your throat, dear."

She broke the connection, held on to the phone, and punched 911.

The two uniformed police officers arrived twenty minutes after the call. Lotte believed that for the department, it was record-breaking time. They thoroughly inspected the house for signs of a break-in. They seemed to know what they were doing.

Officer Bill said, "Locks are intact." His partner, Officer Footer, came in after exploring the outside.

"Windows are locked from the inside. Back door too."

Officer Bill came around from the front door and looked at Lotte. "There doesn't seem to be a break-in, Mrs. Kell."

"Somebody was *in* my house," Lotte said. "They drank my prune juice, for God's sake."

Officer Bill said, "Do you own a cat?"

"Do you *see* a cat?" Lotte said, and watched him look around, as though a cat might be lurking in the house. It made her mad. "There *is* no cat."

"Do you live alone?"

"Yes," Lotte said. "My husband Albert died when I hit menopause."

Officer Bill took the framed picture of a gray-haired man from the low handcrafted china cabinet by the staircase, the man in a camo jacket holding an Uzi submachine gun, and asked her if this was him. Lotte said, "Yes, that's my dear Albert. He loved the outdoors. On his free time he'd go pheasant hunting."

"You can't shoot birds with an Uzi submachine gun."

"Uzi what-gun?" Lotte said. He showed her the picture of her husband she'd forgotten about until now. "Oh. Yes, well, Albert was a crackpot."

Officer Bill placed the picture back on the china cabinet. "Mrs. Kell, does anybody else have the key to the house?"

"Just my youngest granddaughter, Joyce. But she calls if she's coming. And my eldest granddaughter, Joanna. She lives all the way out in Brooklyn. She moved there to get away from New Jersey."

Officer Footer turned his head to Officer Bill and said under his breath, "Or to get as far away from her screwy grandma as the gas in her Miata can take her."

Officer Bill asked with honest curiosity, "Your eldest granddaughter lived in Jersey, did she?"

"No, Manhattan."

Officer Bill had to smile at that—the old woman with her heart in her mouth and still making jokes. He said to her, "Ma'am, the only thing we can do right now is advise you to lock all your windows and doors."

It wasn't good enough. Lotte said, "Excuse me, but your advice is about as useful as my bra. Which I don't have on."

Officer Bill turned to Officer Footer. "I did not need to know that."

"Good day, Mrs. Kell," Officer Footer said, and they started out the door.

Lotte pulled them up short. "So that's it, huh? You're just going to leave? Tell me, Officers Dumb and Dumber, what will you do when you hear that I've been raped and killed in my own home?"

By that time they were at the doorway, a few strides toward the yard, as Officer Footer said to his partner, "I have an answer for her, but not one she'd want to hear."

"Keep it to yourself. At least till we get to the station."

Craig had to think, What idiot introduced my grandma to Spandex? While slumped on the Champ's corner group couch, arms extended along the backrest. With him was his Jamaican American best friend Ray Anderson, a cool guy, but man, he was culinarily challenged. Right now they were watching *Cops* on the 90-inch plasma TV that was mounted on the wall fifteen feet across from them. Watching anything on a big-screen TV was good. Watching it in the man cave of the undisputed heavyweight champion boxer's mansion was paradise. The house was stylishly furnished to suit your comfort, with warm, earthy tones, the best that money could buy, a man-child's playroom with its own pool table, and several Ms. Pac-Man machines. The cave even had its very own minibar. What else could a man want?

It was Ray's choice to watch *Cops* tonight, the loud irritating sirens from the show blared through the sound system and the large speakers into their ears, filling their minds with it. After all, the show was Ray's favorite.

Not Craig's, though. It explained why he was bored out of his fucking mind. "I'm as bored as a blind man in a strip club." He said then, "I'm starting to become very aware of my thoughts." Boredom could do that to you.

With a beckoning motion of a hand Ray said, "Let the thoughts flow out." His bald head gleamed from the overhead light.

"Some idiot introduced my grandmother to Spandex."

Ray made a disgusted face.

"Keep that in there!"

"Oh, I will."

The butler, a tall and lean gentleman who weighed one hundred and sixty, hundred and sixty-two in the tuxedo, had sad eyes, like a servant tired of serving and about to fold away his uniform. The old man's hair was still black by some miracle. Or by *Just for Men* hair dye. He walked into the man cave holding a scoop bucket of water out in front of him lightly, almost gracefully, toward Ray.

"Your bucket of *tap* water, Mr. Anderson."

Ray got up from the corner group couch to receive his bucket, and taking it from him he said, "Good looking out, Butler," almost dropping it.

"My name is *Nood*, sir."

Ray looked at the butler, nonplussed.

"I can't say that while I'm sober."

The butler said, "It's spelled N-double-oh-D."

Ray said, "Yes, but it's pronounced N-U-D-E."

The butler turned up his nose and walked out without saying another word. Man, very touchy.

Craig said to Ray, "You've just made Nood's list." He stood up from the couch and walked toward Ray and the scoop bucket.

For a second there, Ray looked surprised.

"Butler's got a list?"

Craig nodded. "The other day I brought him a basket of chocolate minimuffins for his birthday, and he took my name off the list." He told Ray, "You're right up there with his hairdresser and his tailor."

Ray raised his eyebrows. "You're kidding." Then, in the next moment, he acted hurt, saying, "You got the butler a basket of chocolate minimuffins, and all I got for my birthday was a lousy pack of condoms?"

"Hey, those condoms saved your reputation, man."

Ray let it go. He brought his mind back to the heavy bucket he was holding, dipped his finger, and felt the water's temperature. A shiver ran up his finger, and his arm broke out in goose bumps.

Ray said, "Oh, man, Butler forgot to boil the water. It's ice cold."

Craig said, "Cold works," then took the bucket from him and turned to the three-seater couch where Bobby Piars was passed out. Bobby was the youngest of the three at age twenty two, dimwitted and a screwup. Although kindhearted on occasion, he was often strung out on drugs. He even had a bag of cocaine close to him, a couple of lines already railed on the coffee table. The boy was a miserable sight, beyond repair. The poor bum was trapped in the nineties with the unkempt wavy curls - a white man's excuse for an Afro.

Craig threw the cold water on him. It was a shame junkies didn't wash away like sand.

The ice-cold water jolted Bobby into consciousness. "Jesus Christ!" He looked hard at Ray, then at Craig holding the bucket. Said to him, "Craig? Jesus Christ, what you doing? You wanna drown me in my sleep? Jesus Christ. Couldn't you have thought up a subtle way to wake me up, man? *Jee*-zus Christ."

Craig turned away, not answering, and said to Ray, "That's three times he used the Lord's name in vain."

Bobby came forward onto the edge of the three-seater couch he occupied to himself, to check his coke. His lines were undisturbed.

He said, "You damn lucky you didn't soak up my foo-foo dust."

Foo-foo dust. Craig mused on that.

He said, "Is foo-foo dust like pixie dust?"

Ray took up his place on the corner group couch, turned the TV volume all the way down and said, "Bobby, when you pass out after snorting coke, something's definitely going wrong. I say you figure out what it is. Or else it's going to keep happening . . . God willing."

"I know what it is. You old goats are harshing my buzz."

Craig sat down and placed the bucket between his feet. He said, "Kid, it isn't normal to pass out while snorting cocaine."

"It ain't normal," Bobby said with a big, goofy grin. "It is *awesome*." A glazed look in his eyes, from all that cocaine, the drug working in him.

Craig said to Ray, "You reckon Matt's going to be pissed off we wet his couch?"

"Nah, we'll blame it on Bobby's tiny bladder like we always do."

Bobby frowned. "Hold up—always? How often you blame the couch on me?"

"Not often," Ray said.

And Craig said, "A few ... hundred times is all."

"*What?*" Bobby sprung upright. "Now my brother's gonna think I got a bladder control problem."

Ray was smiling, nodding. "Yes, he does."

"Now that we've revived you," Craig said, "let's see if you can answer the question without crapping out on us again." He locked eyes with the junkie the way he'd look at a slow child, a defective one. "Where is Matt, you *hop*head?"

Bobby moved his shoulders in the hoodie, a lazy shrug.

"Ever since he clapped eyes on that cocktail waitress, Millicent Dallis-Price? He's been camping out at Beatrice Inn. You know, the nightclub that's like a strip club, except the girls there wear clothes?"

Ray said, "He's still stalking her? Why doesn't he just move in for the kill?"

"So why's Matt stalling?" Craig said to Bobby. "Does she have two heads? An extra belly button? *No* belly button?"

"Well, let's put it this way. She's of legal drinking age." Bobby paused for the punchline. "In Cyprus."

Ray was in total disbelief. "No way."

So was Craig. "Come on."

Bobby bent forward over the low table in front of him and snorted off a line of coke. Sitting back he said in ecstasy, "Yeaaah."

Craig smiled broadly, impressed.

"Matt's rocking the cradle."

"I dated a younger girl," Bobby said. "It's no big deal."

"Yeah, but you were both seventeen, whereas Matt is far *from* seventeen." Craig looked at Ray. "What do you know—Matt's gone from patron of the prostitutes to cradle robbing."

"Tell me something, kid," Ray said to Bobby. "Do the white folks in South Africa usually prey on the early birds?"

"We're not animals, Ray. But if a swan approaches a peacock with her breasts leading, the peacock ain't gonna say, 'Up yours.'"

"No," Craig said, "he's going to pea-*cock* that swan."

Ray said he was baffled, and Craig said, "Correction— you're an arrogant jackass."

"Don't question what's out of this world, Irish Dude." Ray's eyes held on Craig as he casually took in the room.

Craig said, "This man cave could use some sprucing up." A stack of sports and mechanics magazines were on the coffee table. Craig went through them, found *Busty Ladies*, and put it on top of the stack. He said, "Better."

"The Champ has never paid this much attention to anyone." A thoughtful frown covered Ray's face, clean-cut, and moderately attractive. "What is it about this girl that's got the big guy going like a couple of Energizer batteries?" He said, "Wait a minute," and then paused and said, "Could it be love?"

Craig said, "Oh yeah," in a tone of skeptic sarcasm. "Every so often I find myself hiding in the bushes outside a girl's house and spying on her through a pair of binoculars because I *love* her."

Bobby passed out on the couch.

Craig looked in the bucket; it was empty. He said, "Damn. Used up all the water."

Ray said, "I've got this," and swiped the TV remote from the table.

Cops was still on. They showed dozens of police cars swarming down the streets of Omaha with sirens blazing. The TV was on mute.

Ray punched the volume to an earsplitting level. Sirens blared out of the speakers and filled up the man cave, snapping Bobby back to consciousness. Bobby assumed the police had come for him, and in his haste to clear up the cocaine, he crashed to the floor and didn't get up again. Stuck there.

They made no move to help him.

As Ray lowered the volume, Craig said to him, "You're the idiot who introduced my grandma to Spandex."

"She asked me to drop her off at her bingo game, and we wound up at your wife's aerobics class."

Lotte woke up from a nap—two in the afternoon, the house quiet—knocked her head on the nightstand and said, "Thank God for the metal plate." She raised her knees and swung her legs off the side of the bed, then slipped her feet into a pair of pink fluffy slippers. She ambled to the end of the hall and stopped. Reaching the top of the staircase she picked up sounds directly below her, the drone of unfamiliar voices.

Strangers in her home.

"Never sit on your child's pet ferret. It'll most likely bite your testicles before dying."

"Well, at least the ferret died with a little bit of dignity."

Talking to each other.

Lotte recoiled from the top of the staircase, startled. "Oh, my *God*."

She hurried back through the hallway to the bedroom and slammed the door.

The intruders raised their gaze to the ceiling as the sound of Lotte's bedroom door closing reached them. The one said, "The old bird's awake." Another told a third to go check on her.

The third started out of the room.

The other two took a swig of their Coors, then stopped as the overhead light began winking in and out. They heard the third intruder counting:

"One … two … three … four …"

"Uh, Conner"—the first intruder looking around at him—"some people find that annoying."

"I was checking to see if the light was working." Realizing he was still flicking the light switch, he stopped. "And yes, they're working."

"Okay. But why were you counting?"

"I wasn't counting."

It was in his voice, the agitation.

"Yes you were. I heard you."

The second intruder said, "I heard you too. And I have headphones on."

"I like to count things. Is that so wrong?"

The first intruder stared at him.

The first intruder said, "Do you have OCD, Conner?"

"I don't know. What's OCD?"

"Obsessive-compulsive disorder. It's when you have the desire to do something over and over and over."

"Sounds like you might have a case of OCD yourself, Owen."

"Having OCD is nothing to be ashamed of. It isn't a horrible thing. It's a *sickness*. Besides," the first intruder said, "you're not alone. A lot of nutty people have OCD."

"Really?"

The one wearing headphones said, "Yeah. As a matter of fact, my wife's cousin was an obsessive-compulsive boozehound. He used to count red cars, and nobody took it seriously."

The third one was intrigued by this information. He said from the door, light switch momentarily forgotten, "So what happened to him?"

"Oh, he died. He was counting and got too close, and a few red cars ran over him."

The third intruder said to the first intruder, "Red cars I am *definitely* not counting," and the first intruder said, "I must say, Conner, I'm surprised. I didn't know you were an obsessive-compulsive nincompoop."

"Why would you? I mean, after all, I went to great lengths to hide it from my family and friends."

The second intruder took off his headphones. "What's your OCD?"

"When I leave the room, I have to flip the light on and off thirteen times, or someone close to me will go to jail."

"Thirteen *times*. Is it really that serious?"

"The last time I walked out a room and forgot to flip the light on and off thirteen times," the third intruder said, "my cousin Jimmy wiped out the mailman." He paused and said, "So yes, I consider my OCD very serious."

Lotte stood there a moment as her hands firmly held the door shut. The intruder's footsteps approached in the hall.

"They're coming." Lotte listened again, then corrected herself and said, "No, only one of them." She listened again and said, "And he walks with the feet of sextuplets."

She desperately looked around for an escape. Lotte slipped into bed. She pulled the covers over her shoulder and pretended to sleep as the intruder came. Seeing her eyes closed and hearing her soft breathing he vacated the bedroom, lightly closing the door on his way out.

The second he was gone, Lotte was out of bed and pacing the room, thinking of what to do, how she was going to get out of this situation.

The phone rang—on the nightstand. She snagged it and then stopped. Lotte held the phone to her ear. Someone was on the downstairs line.

"Come on over," the voice said. "There's plenty of prune juice in the fridge." A fourth intruder.

Lotte lightly placed the phone in the cradle. This was going to be tough. Her route to rescue was, for the meantime, blocked. No. The phone wasn't her only redemption. What else?

The window.

A passage to freedom? Or a plunge toward death?

Lotte turned the lock on the window and opened it to bright sunlight and birds chirping. She leaned out into the breeze and yelled out into the quiet, peaceful afternoon, "Help! Help me! Somebody, please help an old lady out!"

Her cries for the help of her neighbors had the intruders on alert. There were now fifteen of them lounging around and eating out of her fridge.

An intruder in tennis shoes started up the stairs saying, "I'll take care of her." He paused to appraise a ghastly flower wall-pot. "What is the purpose of *that* thing?"

The next door neighbors, Mr. and Mrs. Rogers, settled down to their lunch in front of the TV, were listening to Lotte's cry for help over *Dr. Phil.*

"Somebody call the police! There are in*tru*ders in my house!"

Mrs. Rogers turned her head toward her husband. He was sitting in the recliner with his pants undone, also listening. Right away, he looked at the TV.

"I don't hear a thing," Mr. Rogers said.

The intruder in tennis shoes rushed to Lotte's bedroom and caught her precariously halfway out the window.

Lotte wheeled toward him. She saw that he was holding—a gun.

On his frightening approach Lotte screamed.

"Stay away!"

A small group of Sing Sing inmates sat in the TV room: whites, blacks, and Hispanics together. One inmate stood out from the rest, mainly due to his hair, a red ball of flame. The others called this inmate the Redheaded Negro. He didn't mind the name; he sort of liked it. The name gave him an identity. His parents had christened him Jagger Zuma. He'd last heard from them when he was seven, before they took him deep into the dangerous forest of South Africa and left him there. He had found his way out twenty years later, by then a grown man. With one difference, a head of red hair that conveyed that he was not a normal man. Something in him had changed, for either better or worse.

One thing about Jagger, he was reserved, never raised his voice or got in your face, like some of these color scared motherfuckers sitting around with bug up their asses. Jagger's Capricorn natal sign made him observant; he knew what was going on, rarely missed a beat. There was something mysterious about him. He was a peaceful creature, a simple soul, a meditator.

He sat on a chair next to his friend, a Hispanic named Iggy, watching the championship fight on the small set. The heavyweight boxer, Matthew Piars, had won the championship belt. The commentator's voice announced the victory to the world. "The new undisputed heavyweight champion of the world, Matthew Piars!"

Jagger, staring at Matthew Piars on the TV, quietly said to himself, "Mattie …"

"Was prison like this in South Africa?" Iggy said.

"What you call prison, in South Africa we call the Zoo."

Another inmate took the chair on the other side of Jagger. This one was white, went simply by *Jimmy*, locked up for feeding the mailman to a wood chipper. He was young and often anxious. Usually his type didn't last very long inside; they ended up as somebody's "wife." As of two weeks ago, Jimmy wasn't anybody's wife. His hubby, a three-hundred-pound Canadian bacon, had gotten shanked to death in the exercise yard by a tanked Nazi freak. The catfight was over Jimmy.

Jimmy looked around at the guards before saying to Jagger, "Are you the guy runs the contraband?" in his anxious way. His eyes darted everywhere but at Jagger.

"What do you want?"

"I want an antique radio."

Jagger looked at him. "You're Jimmy." He said to Iggy, "And Jimmy smells of his own piss."

Iggy said, "They put padlocks on his cell 'cause he keeps picking at it with his nails. Till they had to cut it off."

Jimmy held up his hand wrapped in a bandage. "They'll grow back."

"Not without the fingers, they won't," Iggy said. He looked at the TV. "It's called a boxing ring. So shouldn't it be round?"

Jimmy said, "No, 'cause then the boxers'd be running in circles."

Jagger said to Jimmy, "Antique radio, huh? That's hard to come by. Nowadays everything's newly made."

Jimmy put his bandaged hand on Jagger's shoulder. "No, my fellow Redheaded Negro inmate. This one was bought thirty years before you and I came down our mothers' tunnel slides. It belonged to my grandfather. I'd listen to Sinatra on the radio every day after school. That radio was everything to my grandfather. It was his entertainment while he washed in the beer barrel, read the paper on the crapper, and while my grandmother rode his flagpole." He smiled at the memories. "Yeah, that radio's survived through some of the most disgusting times." He said to Jagger, "It's sitting on the dresser in my sister's trailer home in the Bronx as we speak."

"You want *that* radio?"

"I want *that* one." Jimmy paused and said, "Can you get it?" He coaxed Jagger into saying yes. "Last person who said no to me got his head shoved into a wood chipper."

Iggy got into the swing. "You're getting him a radio—I want a sandwich. But not just any old sandwich. This is nine-inch wheat bread topped with succulent strips of mouth-watering steak, chicken breast strips, and bacon. Crowned with delicious meatballs, pepperoni, salami, and ham for a spicy kick. With skipjack tuna, jumbo shrimps and sardines."

The inmates were listening, drooling. A neo-Nazi skinhead's stomach rumbled.

Jimmy swallowed. "They're starving us in here. I could put syrup and ketchup on my pancakes, and it'd still taste better than the crap they feed us in here."

Jagger looked at Iggy. "What, no vegetables?"

Iggy said, "Oh, all right, fine. Put an olive on top."

The warden marched in, right away saying, "Stop what you're doing. Thought you'd want to know, I have banned all contraband activities going on in my prison." He looked at the inmates looking at him, gave them his *don't fuck with me* look, and said, "Whoever you are, your connections have been terminated—so *ha!*" He paused and said, "As you were," and walked out.

Jimmy shook his head and looked at Jagger. "How'll you get my radio without your connections?"

"You'll get your radio."

"I better."

Jagger turned his head.

"There'd better be gold in that radio."

Iggy said to Jagger, "Fuck gold," and then glared at Jimmy and said, "Whitey, there better be *weed*."

Joyce, an unemployed mother at twenty-two, was browsing through the wigs at Sonia Hair Extensions while her-five-month-old daughter slept in her stroller. It was half past one and the clerk's desk was occupied. An African American woman was buying blonde extensions for her hair. There was nothing for Joyce here. Oh, but those red extensions looked good.

The door opened and the baby's deadbeat father came in off the street looking around. Joyce waved him over. Bobby was coming and Joyce leaned over the stroller telling the baby, "Look, Poppy, it's Daddy."

Bobby reached them and said, "How much you got in your purse?"

"A fifty-dollar bill and two bucks worth of tampons."

Bobby made a face, an expression of disgust, at the mention of tampons.

He recovered and said, "I need the fifty."

"What for?" The girl suspicious.

Bobby hesitated. "I need it for … supplies, let's say."

Joyce could always tell when he was lying. It was easy; he lied whenever he was awake. And often the lies were about him needing money for a fix.

She said, "I'm not giving you money to buy foo-foo dust."

"So what you're basically telling me is," Bobby said, "you not gonna give me the fifty."

Joyce went in her canvas bag hanging on the back of the stroller. She produced a bill and handed it to him.

Bobby looked at the blue fifty-dollar bill. "This is Monopoly money."

"The other day when I asked you for a glass of water? You gave me your shoe."

"What," Bobby said, "you never drank out of a shoe?"

This guy was either dumb or uncomfortable being in a wig shop.

"You're not getting a real fifty from me." Joyce crossed her hairy arms under her small, ample breasts, like she'd made up her mind and there was nothing he could say that would change her decision.

"Fine, be a tight-fisted bitch," Bobby said. "If you not gonna give me the fifty, then I'm taking your baby."

"She's your baby too."

"Oh, yeah." Bobby paused and said, "Still works. I'm taking her." He took his daughter from the coziness of her stroller and, having been rudely awaken from her nap, she started crying. Bobby walked out of the wig store, holding

22

the baby close to his chest, as if making off with a bag of loot.

Joyce yelled after him in panic, "Bobby!"

The poor girl stood there—scared stiff, and indecisive. "Oh God."

A police squad car was turtled into a junction facing Main Street, its engines and sirens off.

Across the way to the other side, Joyce, in an olive green parka coat, unstrapped, wandered aimlessly along the sidewalk. Inside the squad car Officer Bill's sharp eyes spotted her immediately. He said, "Look at that."

Officer Footer stirred, sat up straighter. He said, "Where?"

Officer Bill said, "Where I'm *loo*king." Officer Footer followed Officer Bill's gaze to the dazed young woman. "Anything about that stroller strike you as odd?"

"Yeah. What's the difference between prams and strollers?"

"We'll pick that topic up later. What I meant was that there's no baby in it."

They watched the young woman step into a phone booth and lift the receiver. She punched in some numbers and right away hung up without speaking. Next she went into a convenience store and used the pay phone. She dialed three numbers they didn't see and listened to a voice they didn't hear. She again hung up without talking.

Bill and Footer exchanged a quizzical look.

Joyce came out of the convenience store, pushing the empty stroller. Still in a daze, she walked away.

Officer Bill said, "That was strange," and Officer Footer agreed, nodding.

"Yeah."

Their voices drifting with a thoughtful sound to it.

Officer Bill popped his door open. He said to Footer, "Come on," and they got out of the car and split up. Officer Bill went to the phone booth and dialed the last call made. He got the voice of a 911 operator.

"911 operator. What's your emergency?"

On the convenience store pay phone, Footer was also listening to the voice of a 911 operator.

"911 operator. State your emergency."

Bill stepped out of the phone booth and met up with Footer, Footer walking out of the convenience store. They lost sight of the dazed young woman and the empty stroller.

CNN was on.

Ray and Craig had draped their jackets over the arm and back of the couch. They were prepared to go out.

Ray picked up the TV remote. He said, "Let's see what's on the Islam Channel."

CNN switched to the Islam Channel. Three dark-bearded, turban-wearing Muslims, seated on a sofa, were engaged in a religious debate.

"The man is claiming to be a prophet," the Muslim host said. "He said he has revelations coming to him from the heavens. That means you need to know if he's really a prophet."

Ray was on the edge of his seat, listening intently, trying to follow every word. "If I spoke Arabic, I'd understand what they were saying."

"They're speaking English," Craig said.

The man of the house walked in—Bobby's older brother, Matthew "Matt" Piars, the six-five, two-hundred-and-fifty-two-pound fighter. Matthew was a sharp-suited tycoon in a two-thousand-dollar pair of shoes. Underneath all that height, weight, and wealth was a charming, affectionate, fear-inspiring fighter. Though Matthew was a white man, he was a different kind of white man, a dark-skinned Caucasian. Or else very tanned. His skin was not the kind of skin you often found among Europeans, this white man could only have come out of South Africa.

As if on cue, fireworks exploded on the plasma screen.

Matthew looked at the TV. "What's wit' the fireworks? Is the president dead?"

Ray said, "Some cheerleader snuck fireworks into the school and lit 'em in the cafeteria. Go, team spirit!"

"We ready to go?" Craig said, on his feet now.

"Hold on," Matthew said. "Is my mistakenly born little brother back from the wig shop?"

Craig said, "No," and said, "But hey, Matt, let's just go without him," his voice low, confidential. "The kid doesn't need to know where we went."

"Hey, Matt," Ray said. He got Matthew's attention. "Monica Bellucci in full frontal nudity."

Now Matthew looked busy thinking about it, no doubt the big guy was picturing a naked Monica Bellucci in his head that was made of steel, the head that in the boxing ring took fourteen rounds of beatings.

"Thanks for that image, Ray," Matthew said, nodding in appreciation. "That'll help me weave around the stupid student drivers without ramming 'em off the road."

Craig said, "Great. Now we don't have to wear our seat belts."

"Good," Ray said. "I hate wearing seat belts."

"I know," Matthew said. "Aside from securing your date to your lap while she rides you as you drive, seat belts are totally useless."

Then came the faint sound of a baby wailing its head off. Matthew and Ray looked at the TV, the volume low. The crying wasn't coming from the TV.

Craig had a look on his face that got his eyes wide open and made him appear rigid standing there, like something frightened him. "Oh no," he said. "It's happening. I'm having that dream again."

The three men turned to the doorway as the crying got closer. Bobby came in, carrying his five-months-old daughter. The baby was bawling in the drug addict's trembling arms.

Matthew looked straight at Bobby now, frowning a little, like he was trying to make sense of this picture.

"Young blood?"

Bobby said, "Help," with real desperation.

"What are you doing wit' the baby?" Matthew said. "I thought the judge said you couldn't hold her without a chaperone."

"I took the baby from Joyce."

A pained expression came over Craig's face. "Ooh," he said, "that does not sound good."

Matthew was outraged. "You did—you did *what*?"

Ray said, "Matt, what's South African for dumb ass?"

"Joyce will get the baby back," Bobby said, "when she gives me fifty dollars."

It came to Matthew all at once. He said, "You're holding your daughter for ransom?"

"*Jee*-zus Christ," Ray said.

Craig turned to Ray next to him. "The kid can't seriously be that stupid." Heard Bobby answer Matthew with, "Just till I get the fifty," and Ray said to Craig, "Evidently he can."

"Young blood …" Matthew socked his little brother hard across the head. "What the fuck is wrong wit' you?"

"Ah—" Bobby's hand flew to his head. "Easy, bro!" He adjusted his grip on the wailing baby. "I get the money, I'll give it back to Joyce."

Jesus, every time he opened his mouth shit came out.

Craig stepped in. "Matt, I'll handle this."

He approached Bobby. Craig was the understanding, rational type. Gave you the feeling you could talk to him. His social demeanor was welcoming. He had green eyes to match his Irish background, light hair that looked like he groomed with his fingers. You wouldn't see him wearing anything beyond casual attire, made do with his closet full of jeans, T-shirts and sweaters he wore with sneakers, the man always wore sneakers, no matter the occasion—even wore sneakers to funerals. He didn't have much size to him—was stringy, but could have been an athlete at one time. In his other life.

"Bobby," Craig said, more tolerant of the fool. "Listen, kid. You're shacking up with my wife's little sister. In Ireland, that makes you pretty much family. So I'm gonna give it to you straight."

As Craig said "straight," he made an upward motion with his forefinger. Bobby tracked the finger, like a patient tracking the movement of an optician's light. Craig kept motioning with his finger and Bobby's bloodshot eyes kept tracking its movement.

Craig stared a moment and then turned to Matthew and Ray. He said, "We're wasting time. Let's go."

The three older men started out of the room, Matthew saying, "Alright, but how long is this barbecue at your in-laws' place gonna be? I have a date wit' Millicent, and I intend to pick her up and watch her booty-walk to my brand-new Jag."

Ray touched his arm. "Wait up."

They were at the man cave doorway.

"You made the kill?"

"I'm taking her for drinks in London."

Craig said, "When I want to get high, I go to Amsterdam."

"And then after drinks," Matthew said, "I'm going to fly her back to New York and drop her off at her place and then …"

"Go home friend-zoned?" Craig said.

"Feed on the carcass, Champ"—Ray bumping fists with Matthew—"feed on it *good*."

Bobby didn't like being forgotten. "Whoa, whoa, whoa … *whoa*."

Craig returned a stultified look.

"You're still here?"

Bobby said, "*Yuh*," and said, "You guys gonna help me with this screaming imp?"

All he wanted to know.

Ray said, "He's gone from calling the baby *it* to *imp*."

"Taking care of a screaming baby," Craig said, "isn't really on my to-do list, Bob."

Bobby turned pleading eyes to Matthew.

"Bro?"

Matthew said to his little brother, the big-time screwup, "You made the baby, now burp it."

The older three men started out again.

"But I don't know *how*," Bobby telling this to Matthew, Ray and Craig as he watched them walking off.

They turned into the hall.

"There ought to be a law on who should and should not reproduce," Craig said. "Maybe someday there will."

Ray ogled the maid, a good-looking brunette in a gray uniform, the skirt inches above her knees, as she walked by them in the hall.

Ray glanced down at his pants, where the crotch bulged, and said, "Down, boy … she's *way* too young for you."

Jagger stood looming in the front room of the trailer, three hours out of prison. Right away he located the antique radio, on the dresser. The radio was held together with glue and duct tape, ineptly applied, after many years of use as a bludgeon over Jimmy's head by his grandfather. Jagger said, "Come on—I broke out of prison for this piece of shit?"

Right then, Joyce walked in the door to see the prisoner in her house. Her early arrival stopped him.

"Who are you? And what are you doing in my house?" Joyce came at him with a lamp, mouth twisted in a snarl of rage, sorrow in her swollen red eyes, cheeks flushed, Joyce screaming, "Leave my house!"

"Whoa!" Jagger dodged the lamp. "Swing 'em, cowgirl!" He said, "I can explain. If you'd just let me—easy with that thing!"

"*Leave.*"

Jagger's eyes happened on the empty stroller. "Say, where's your baby?"

As if he'd struck a chord, Joyce paused with the lamp in midstrike over her head. She broke down in tears and fell into him. Jagger held the young woman awkwardly in his arms.

She was clean. Something he wasn't use to.

Lotte grabbed a wooden-backed chair, an old one, belonged to her mother, a gift crafted by an abusive carpenter, her father. She raised her mother's chair and threatened to use it on the intruder in her room.

"Stay back," Lotte said. "I'm double-warning you."

The intruder moved toward her, started to motion—with the gun—and Lotte heaved the chair at him, driving him back out of her bedroom.

The chair hit the wall and snapped. She imagined her dear, departed father turning in his grave, all his hard work gone to ruin.

"Sorry, Dad," Lotte said, in prayer, as her eyes went to the ground.

Jagger leaned his rear against the edge of the table listening to Joyce's revelation of her day. "Hold on," Jagger said, once he'd heard enough. "Let me see if I've got this straight. Your crackhead boyfriend kidnapped his daughter, from his girlfriend, for a measly fifty bucks?"

"Messed up, right?"

Jagger said, "A tad bit, yeah. He could've aimed a little higher." She gave him a look and he apologized, then had to wait a moment, thinking what kind of father would kidnap his own child, and said, "Forget the police," conjuring up a plan. "Call your boyfriend's brother."

The brother. Of course. Why hadn't she thought of that? If anybody could talk some sense into Bobby, it was his fear-inspiring older brother.

Joyce reached over and brought the corded telephone to her, on the same table she ate breakfast, lunch and dinner. Jagger watched her pick the receiver, hold it to her ear and dial a number with calloused, hard-working hands. Her nails could use a manicure. She wore a checked shirt with jeans, her hair in a ponytail. This was a woman who had no time for herself, spent most of it taking care of the baby of a useless man.

"Put the call on speaker," Jagger said.

Anxious to hear the Champ's voice, Jagger pushed up onto the table and propped his soiled shoes on the seat of the chair to listen closely.

The line rang …

And rang.

They were at a backyard barbecue. Matthew took his time to retrieve his noisy cell phone from the inner breast pocket of his blazer. Once he had it out he looked at the caller ID. It told him: *Joyce is calling.*

Matthew looked up as realization dawned. "Oh, my right foot has no sock. How did I *miss* that?"

He answered the call.

"Piars."

Jagger, seated on the table, elbows on his knees and his hands clasped at his mouth, said quietly to himself, "Mattie."

As Joyce was saying, "Matt, it's me. Have you spoken to Bobby?"

Matthew said, "Crap." His voice sounding faint then, away from the phone, and they heard him say, "Joyce's asking 'bout Bobby. Think she's onto us." Matthew's full voice came back saying, "Bobby? Yeah, he came by the manse wit' the baby."

Joyce right away said, "Is she okay? Hold on a sec." She rebuked Jagger: "That is not a footstool—that is a chair."

Jagger, like a bad-mannered child, quickly took his dirty deck shoes off the seat.

"The baby's fine," Matthew said, "although she was screaming bloody murder. Christina Aguilera ain't got nothin' on her."

Joyce glanced at Jagger. She was young, barely a woman, and already had crow's feet at the corners of her eyes. He motioned for her to hang up.

Matthew was saying, "You coming to the barbecue?"

"We'll see how I'm feeling when I hang up," Joyce said, then put the phone down and shrugged, dispassionate, "Meh."

"Don't call the police," Jagger said. "Or your lawyer. I have no doubt your boyfriend will bring the baby back. Hopefully the baby and not a trash bag full of soiled diapers."

"You sound sure that he will. Almost as if"—Joyce cautious now, careful with this runaway prisoner—"it takes one to know one."

"He's as impatient as you say he is, he won't be able to stand the baby's crying." He looked at Joyce and said, "You understand?"

No, she didn't, and shook her head.

"The crying will irritate him, drive him nuts till he gives up and brings her back. We'll give him till tomorrow morning. I guarantee it'll be the first thing he'll do."

It sounded good, except for one thing.

Joyce said it. "You're forgetting we're dealing with a drug addict."

Jagger paused to consider this and then said, "Okay, the second thing he'll do."

Wailing sirens approached up the street and then cut off as it stopped in front of Lotte Kell's house.

One of the intruders edged to the front window and peered out to see two uniformed police officers get out of the squad car, holsters loaded with automatics.

"Oh, fuck. She actually managed to call the police."

The one with OCD didn't like how this was turning out. "I said this was a bad idea, and see, I was right."

The doorbell rang.

The one at the front window went to deal with the police.

Lotte was crouched quietly at her bedroom door, her breath held, listening to her intruders talk to the police officers. It gave her hope.

"Everything okay, officers?"

Listening to them, waiting for an answer.

It came from one of the officers. "Your neighbors reported someone calling for help. A Mrs. Lotte Kell?" Not sounding too sure of his information.

"Uh yes, it was our, ah, grandmother … If you have to know."

And hope vanished.

"No," Lotte said from her place at her bedroom door. "I don't know these people."

"Is that her?"

This coming from the other police officer, becoming curious of the old lady upstairs, her tiny voice drifting down the floor separating them.

"That's her," the intruder said through nervous laughter, then called out to her, "I'll be right with you, Nana!" He said to the officers at the front door, "You see, officers, she's a little … on the cuckoo side."

Lotte couldn't keep quiet. These lies they were saying about her, made it impossible to hold herself back.

"No! No! No!"

The first officer, the talker of the two, said, "Keep the noise to a minimum."

"We will, officers. To a minimum. Bye-bye now."

"No, don't go!" Lotte called as she heard the front door close, "Come back! Get these intruders out of my house!" She said, "Goddamn it! There goes Dumb and Dumber's even dumber twins."

The intruder exhaled deeply after dealing with the police. That was a close one.

Lotte rose from behind the bedroom door. Her hand gripped the knob and turned it counterclockwise. The door didn't open. She jiggled frantically on the knob. The door still wouldn't budge. It was locked.

"They locked me in."

She had to get out of the house and her only escape was the window.

Lotte looked out to gauge how far it was to the ground. A good twenty-foot drop. Twenty-feet was all it would take to kill a seventy-eight year old woman, break every brittle bone in her frail old body. She watched a crow swoop down and grab a squirrel in its talons, and kept watching as it flew away with the squirrel. Lotte wheeled to face the room, the door, the closet, and the unmade bed. "I need a rope." She thought for a moment and said, "I don't have a rope, so I guess I'll have to make one."

She stared at her bed, at the rumpled sheets.

Hmmmm.

It took her a few minutes to tie the sheets together to make a rope, leaving the bed bare. It was still a few feet too short. She needed more sheets.

Lotte poked through her closet and her foot, bare, stepped on something. It felt loose. She checked it out. Moving stuff out of the way she came upon a loose floorboard. Under it was her late husband's Uzi submachine gun and everything that came with it. Staring at it she became hypnotized by the weapon. "A gun …" She blinked then, uncertain. "That *is* a gun, right?"

She put the magazine in the Uzi. Forty bullets. Which was more than enough. Lotte tried a few tentative steps toward the bedroom door.

"Time to clean up the house."

Her hand touched the knob and turned it clockwise. The door opened willingly.

She stepped out into the hallway. Someone came out of the room across from her. An intruder. Female.

Saying to Lotte, "Are you feeling more cooperative now?"

Lotte didn't say anything. She aimed and fired lethal rounds into the intruder's chest in three seconds. For an old bat, she didn't have a bad aim. Then the recoil of the Uzi made her drop it.

Lotte, picking up the Uzi, said, "Oh, dear me."

She ventured through the hallway with the Uzi, running into more of them. They came out at her from every angle.

"What the fuck?" Seeing his dead friend in the hall.

The Uzi spewed bullets. It put him down.

Another came at her. "Christ!" The Uzi kicked bullets into him, and he spasmed and hit the floor.

The intruders downstairs panicked at the sound of gunshots.

"Jesus Christ!"

The Uzi spat out more bullets upstairs.

Somebody bounded down the stairs. "She found Grandpa's Uzi, and she's taking out the entire gene pool!"

Screaming it, frightened.

Somebody else said, "Fucking hell."

Lotte was pissed. She refused to be kept hostage in her own home. She went on a shooting rampage through the house. It was like shooting ducks at a county fair.

A voice came from the racket, "Keep the children outside!"

There are so many of them, Lotte thought. Where did they all *come* from?

"When I say get out of my house," Lotte said, firing the Uzi, "I mean get out of my house! I don't mean make yourselves at home! Or listen to music! Or eat my food and drink my prune juice! I mean get *out* of my *house*!"

Lotte took them all down. They were sprawled around in the kitchen, on the stairs, in the halls and the living room. Once they were all down, Lotte plunked down on the sofa. Frightened and exhausted, she sobbed.

She gave herself time to settle her nerves. Then raised her head and her gaze came upon a photo album on the coffee table, open. Lotte took her time and looked through it, something to do while the neighbors concluded that the sounds they heard weren't backfires and reported the shots to the authorities.

Lotte frowned. Something wasn't right.

In the family photo album, she noticed the faces of her intruders. They were posing with her.

Lotte drooped.

"No ... no ..."

They were hugging her. One was caught in the action of pecking her on the cheek. She shook her head. This can't be.

"No, no, no, no." Her voice was low, vehement.

Lotte closed her eyes, hard, and opened them again, as though to clear this trickery from her vision. She denied what she was seeing in the photo album.

"They had guns," Lotte said. "They had *guns*, for God's sake."

She looked at the bodies of the intruders. They bled out on her rug. Some were still clutching their handguns. Why hadn't they used them on her when she was killing them?

Wait a minute now.

She blinked.

They weren't guns. They were water pistols.

Children were crying in the backyard. Lotte crossed the room to the window and looked out into her garden. The rest of the family and friends were having a barbecue.

Matthew, Ray and Craig were among the horrified faces looking at her looking at them. The worst were the children. Terrified, they goggled at her.

"Nana . . ."

Lotte felt woozy from the adrenaline. She gave her head a brisk shake that did more harm than good, causing her to stagger. She held onto the window ledge to keep herself steady.

Something was in the pocket of her nightgown. She took it out. It was a bottle of medication, pills prescribed by her doctor. On the side label it read: *Aricept*.

Lotte began to comprehend that she might have known these people. People she had mercilessly gunned down. The clouds cleared away, and events started to make sense again. The intruders calling her Nana. The misguided water pistols. Turning her bedroom doorknob the wrong way and then the right way. The growing number of them. Her family and friends were throwing a barbecue. Her grandchildren and great-grandchildren had been playing squirt guns with the adults.

Lotte said, "They were *family*."

She hadn't remembered their faces or the barbecue because her Alzheimer's hadn't allowed her.

Those in the garden watched Lotte retreat from the window, humiliation in her amber, aged eyes. Next they heard the Uzi go off again as the old and sick woman rubbed herself out of existence.

Craig howled. "Nana!"

The men left what they were doing and ran in the house.

It was the following morning.

Joyce and Jagger were awake drinking coffee. Jagger's cup went untouched. Joyce telling him, "I kicked Bobby out. Couldn't stand the sight of him in his undies and scratching his ass. Stashing weed in the battery box of the TV remote." She sipped her coffee. "So he's been staying with his brother in the Hamptons."

Jagger, still in his prison attire, TV remote idly in hand, glanced at the news: a domestic violence that had turned homicidal. Nothing about a prison escape. He had been out for over fourteen hours and nobody at Sing Sing was aware that he was gone. There were over a thousand inmates behind that razor wire—who could keep count? He smiled, proud of his brilliant escape, and said to the TV, "Bunch of clueless motherfuckers."

Then the expectant knock came on the door.

Jagger and Joyce looked at each other.

Now Jagger was out of his chair and at the small window by the door. Bobby stood at the trailer's small stoop. He had brought the baby back. The traumatized infant was bawling and shedding tears.

Joyce waited.

Jagger looked at her and nodded. That was all she wanted to know. Joyce rushed to the door and yanked it open to her baby crying. Yesterday that crying had been an unbearable sound. Now it was welcome. Bobby, on the other hand, looked like he'd suffered the brunt of it. She almost felt sorry for him.

Bobby, subdued now, said, "Keep the fifty," handed the baby back to Joyce, and then tottered off.

Joyce closed the door, glad to see the back of her worthless drug addict of a boyfriend. Even more glad to have her bundle of joy. She said, "Everything's okay," in a quiet tone, soothing. "You're with Mommy now."

Back in the familiar arms of her mother, the baby gradually stopped crying.

Joyce looked at Jagger.

Jagger smiled with his white teeth.

He was seated at the table, the antique radio next to him. Joyce came out of the next room and quietly closed the door.

"She's sound asleep," Joyce giggled. "I'm so—" She kept giggling. "I'm sorry, I can't—" More giggles came out of her. "I can't seem to stop laughing. Oh, God, I'm just so happy to have her back."

"I can see that. It sounds like you inhaled a whole tank of laughing gas." Jagger held up a sandwich wrapped in foil. "Hope you don't mind I made a snack to go."

The battery compartment on the back of the TV remote was open and empty.

"That's absolutely and positively fine. Listen," Joyce said, "I want to thank you for helping me through this difficult time."

"Don't mention it."

"If it weren't for you, I wouldn't have known what to do." She held his eyes for a few moments, looking to see what she might find in there. She said, "You're such a nice man. Which brings up an interesting question. Why were you in prison?"

Jagger told her it was a long and twisted tale.

"You broke out."

"I wanted to see the world and how much of it has changed."

She floundered. She said wow. "How long were you in prison?"

"Six weeks."

Joyce frowned now, noticing something about him.

"Why do you glow?"

Jagger said, "Sometimes ghosts give off light." Fixing Joyce with a deadpan gaze.

It stopped her. "Did you just say . . . *ghost*?"

Jagger held his blank expression, then his mouth stretched into a slow, pleasant grin. Kidding with her. Joyce threw her head back and laughed.

"I don't know why I glow," Jagger said. "I think it's the soap they let us use."

"It's not that noticeable."

"Good to know."

Joyce said, "You don't mind me asking …" She was unsure how to phrase her next question. "What did you do to get put behind bars?"

"I cut my mother up into six pieces." This time he didn't grin.

Joyce gave him an open-mouthed look now, shocked.

Jagger pushed up from the table in his green prison scrubs, picked up the antique radio and the sandwich. He said, "Thanks for the radio," then walked out.

Joyce stared after him, not moving.

Jimmy sat in his one-man cell in Sing Sing, listening to music on his grandfather's antique radio, emotional yet gratified.

Iggy lay down on the bed in his own cell, and as his head hit the pillow, he felt something under it. He slipped a hand between the pillow and the mattress. Whatever it was, it was big. Wrapped in foil.

Iggy lifted the pillow. It was his nine-inch sandwich.

He said, "Son of a bitch got it."

Iggy sat up and eagerly examined his sandwich.

"Everything in here? Steak, chicken breasts, bacon … Oh yeah, meatballs. Pepperoni. Salami and ham, hell yeah. Skipjack tuna, jumbo shrimps and, oh, *sardines*."

There should be more. Iggy's expression softened when he couldn't find it.

"Where's the olive?"

Right there on top of the sardines, disguised in plastic. Iggy pulled on the plastic and what came out was a dime bag of marijuana.

Iggy bounced giddily on his rear going, "Hee-hee," like a little girl, then saying, "Fucking Redheaded Negro cracked the code!"

KICKED OUT OF HEAVEN

They were in Matthew's three-year-old Jaguar sedan, spotless, the car shining in the dusk's early light, on their way home. Bobby talkative all the way down Columbus Avenue, saying, "In my opinion, old people in Africa are healthier, stronger, and live longer. Illnesses such as Alzheimer's, cancer, arthritis and Parkinson's disease are uncommon in Africa. Ask yourself—why is that? 'Cause in Africa there are fruits and vegetables that ain't meant to be eaten, and yet we eat 'em here. And as a result, we First World countries are left with long-term effects." He dipped into the grocery bag on his lap. "Take this cucumber, for instance. In Africa, we don't eat cucumbers."

Matthew, looking at him as he drove, said, "All I asked was for you to put your seat belt on."

Bobby put his seatbelt on, then commenced fiddling with Matthew's phone. "Bro, you got voicemail from your foster dad."

"Play it."

Bobby put the voicemail on speaker. Both men listened to the man who, fifteen years ago, had fostered Matthew when he was a fourteen-year-old white immigrant thousands of miles away from his home and family in South Africa, a runaway who stole the cold heart of Manhattan's most powerful criminal court judge, Vincent Gray Murphy.

"I said testimonies, not testicles," Vincent Murphy said to someone with him, and then said into the phone, "Son, call me back."

Bobby said, "That's weird."

Matthew said no. "That's normal."

Bobby looked out his window. He said, "That's the market the cat lady buys her food."

"What kind of cats does she have?"

Bobby looked over. "Sixty-*five*."

Matthew slowed down at the crosswalk. He got out and Bobby watched him assist an old, bent woman across the street, Matthew the gentleman. Bobby rolled his eyes. That's three minutes of his life his brother's gone and wasted.

Matthew got the old woman safely to the other side, and she thanked him by saying, "I sleep topless."

She was flirting, having fun with him, this eighty-five-year-old woman, and it surprised Matthew, Matthew who wasn't expecting it. She wobbled away.

Matthew said, "That ought to teach me to help old ladies cross the street."

He turned to go back to the Jaguar and was looking into the face of an attractive woman who had been standing right there watching. She was so close he could smell her perfume. Something flowery. Jasmine.

She said, "Aren't you the gentlemen?" When she saw his white gold wedding ring her smile didn't fade, but it did weaken. "Are there more like you at home?"

Bobby impatiently yelled from the Jaguar, "Come on, bro, let's fucking go!"

Killing the mood. Matthew gave the attractive woman a winsome smile, got in the Jaguar and drove away toward the Hamptons.

Back living with his girlfriend now for three years, Bobby was crashed on the tattered sofa stoned out of his mind. Joyce walked in the door with Poppy to see that her pathetic baby Daddy hadn't moved since she left two hours ago for the store.

Poppy, now three and a half, said, "Hi, Daddy." She didn't care if her father was a loser, she still loved him.

Bobby didn't get up from the sofa. He moved his head to look at them, surprised.

"What you doing with her?"

Joyce said, "I left her with Sadie."

"I thought she was here. I put food out for her."

The food, a single raw carrot on a plate on the table, that a runaway prisoner once sat on thirty six months ago.

"You call an unwashed raw carrot food?" Joyce said.

"Hey, to a rabbit that's breakfast, lunch and dinner."

"Are you comparing our daughter to a rabbit?"

Bobby said, "Rabbits are cute."

"All right, that's it," Joyce said. She set the groceries on the table and turned back to him in a different mood now—arms folded across her breasts, irritable. "Bobby, we have to talk."

"We are talking."

"I want you to move out."

Bobby made a sound like, Ugh. This again? He said, "Joyce, you really gotta come up with an original conversation starter."

"Perhaps I need to make myself a little clearer." Joyce enunciated, "I am breaking up with you."

"What? Why?"

Bobby pulled a wounded face. Maybe he was, and maybe he was putting it on. Either way it didn't matter to Joyce.

"I want a good man," Joyce said, "and I want a good father for Poppy. And you're neither."

"I was good enough to knock you up."

Joyce stood firm. "It's over."

"Come on, I can change—and I will. Starting from next Wednesday, you'll see me change … from this sofa to the table."

"Why next Wednesday?"

"'Cause that's how long the coke will last me for."

"I want you out of the trailer."

"I ain't going nowhere. This is my trailer too." Bobby paused and said, "How bad is this? We're fighting over a trailer."

Joyce said, "Okay, I didn't want to tell you." She mustered courage and let it out. "I've been seeing someone else, and I plan for him to move in. But first you gotta *move out.*"

It stopped him as it hit him where it hurt most, his average-sized dick.

"You seeing someone?" He paused and said, "Oh, I wish you hadn't told me. Now I'm gonna have to beg you to let me stay, and it ain't gonna be pretty."

She had his clothes, his bong and his needle packed into a trash bag and was preparing to throw them outside when he clung to her ankle, begging for another chance, Joyce dragging him along like a ball and chain. "Read my lips," Joyce said. "*No more chances.* Haven't you heard a word I said?"

"I heard every thousand and twelve words you said to me since you walked in the trailer with our rabbit …"

"Then why're you acting stupid?"

"And I'm catching up to the other fifty," Bobby said. And a moment later said, "I'm not stupid."

Her new boyfriend's name was Chris, and he was no different from Bobby—also an addict, an alcoholic. She really knew how to pick them.

They were in his studio apartment, with a view of the alley where a hobo slept in a cardboard box beside a dumpster. Bobby was no different from the hobo either. Few years ago he was right where the hobo was, an illegal alien out of South Africa who had come to America in search of his runaway older brother. Still, an alcoholic was better than a hobo and a junkie. For starters, Chris had his own apartment; though it was small, they had privacy. She just wished she knew where everything was.

"Where is the bread?"

Chris said, "In the freezer." Like where else would he keep a bread.

She fetched the bread from the freezer and came back to the counter. "Where's the bread knife?"

"Bread knife—shit. Joyce, just use any old knife."

"And where *are* the knives?"

"If there's none in the sink, then check the utensil drawer."

Joyce opened drawers until she found the utensils, not in a drawer where he said it would be but in a cardboard box. She opened the cupboard door and found it underneath the sink.

"Joyce, what are you doing?"

"Making us a snack."

"A minute ago you said you was gonna do the laundry."

Joyce took the bread knife from the cardboard box of utensils. She closed the cupboard door, then sighed as she straightened.

"I couldn't find the detergent."

"I keep it in the fridge," Chris said.

"You keep your laundry detergent in the fridge?"

"This is a studio apartment, there's not much space around here. Besides, keeping the detergent in the fridge is what makes my clothes smell so fresh."

"At my place I know where everything is."

"Let's go to your place."

"We can't," Joyce said. "Not with Bobby still crawling around there."

"He hasn't moved out?"

Joyce shook her head saying no. "He's chained himself to the sofa and the TV."

"Tell him to leave."

"I have. Would you like to see his carpet burns where I dragged him by my ankle?"

Chris walked to the counter where Joyce was chopping tomatoes on a chopping board, a bowl of lettuce and diced cucumber next to the sink. He said, "You want me to tell him?"

He watched Joyce think about it before raising her eyebrows. She said, "Send the new boyfriend to dump the old boyfriend," and said, "That's a catfight waiting to happen."

It was only a couple hours later Chris got back.

He said, "It's taken care of."

Joyce turned off the TV. "He moved out?"

"Yep."

Chris took off his coat. He hung it up and sat with her, Joyce making room for him on the sofa. "All right, take me through," Joyce said. "What happened?"

"What you said, he moved out."

"There were no fights?"

"Don't flatter yourself, Joyce. You're not that big a prize."

Joyce let it go. She had gone through eight boyfriends in her lifetime and taken insults from each one. She had learned not to take it personally.

Joyce had her next question ready and asked it. "How did you get him to leave?"

"Well, you know when you told me he chained himself to the sofa and the TV? He really did, he chained himself to the sofa and the TV. And he said if I found the key to the chains, he'd move out."

Joyce knew better. "He misplaced the key, didn't he?"

"I had to help him look for it."

"Where was it?"

"Buried in his Afro curls. Had to pick it out like it was monkey lice."

"Bobby hides everything in his Afro. It's how he was able to walk on those drug possession charges."

"They don't think to look in the hair, do they?"

"No," Joyce said. Then was curious, asking, "But how did you know to look in his hair?"

"Considering he was chained up, it was the only place he could reach."

"What if the key had been in his pants?"

Chris turned his head to Joyce. "All my energy is going into not thinking about it."

This was Jagger and Iggy's spot on the bleachers. It gave them a clear view of the prison yard, inmates getting in fresh air and some exercise, smoking and playing basketball. The ball a beanbag somebody had made in textiles.

Jagger said, "Goddamn screws took away my phone privileges."

"So you wake up and decide you going to see the Champ," Iggy said. "You going to visit the undisputed heavyweight champion, the entrepreneur, by breaking out of prison again?" He said to Jagger, "What'd the Champ do to you?"

"You're dying to know how I do it, aren't you?"

"I was you, I'd dig my way out with a plastic spoon."

"Plastic spoons break, Iggy."

"Then I'd tunnel out with my teeth. Who gives a damn? I'm getting the fuck outta here."

Jagger looked at him. "With that attitude, Iggy, you may make it halfway."

"Damn," Iggy said. He had to think on it before saying, "I know how you do it."

Jagger turned his head and looked at him. "Don't kid yourself."

"Oh, I know how," Iggy said. "With toilet paper, razor blade, a towel, and toothpaste."

"Are you trying to break out of prison or into a gas station bathroom?"

"All right, I give up. How are you getting out?"

Jagger eyeballed the prison yard with its razor wire fence and guard tower. He said, "There's only one way out of this shit hole."

The whistle blew piercingly as a desperate inmate, who went by the name of Pits, ran up the razor wire fence like Spider-Man.

Iggy said, "Ah, look-it. Pits's got the right idea."

Jagger watched with everybody as Pits got six feet off the ground—inmates cheering—and then was shot off the fence. He dropped like a dead fly.

"Then again," Jagger said, "some ideas are only good in your head."

"Sorry we won't be at the arena to watch you fight, Matt. But know," Ray said, "I'm not going to take my eye off the screen for one second."

"While the other eye looks up the French maid's skirt?"

Ray came around the pool table and bent over his cue stick. He glanced up and said, "Man, is there a day that goes by you don't have a drink in your hand?" to Craig watching them play pool. The Irishman stood by, a cold Guinness in his hand, wearing a white T-shirt over faded jeans and socks, no shoes. Feeling right at home.

Craig raised the bottle and took a long chug of his beer. Lowering the bottle he said, "Nope. Haven't come to that day yet."

Matthew watched his hopeless little brother come in without greeting them and sink onto the couch on his spine. The kid was beaten beyond recognition and was still walking.

Matthew looked toward the hall, then back to Bobby.

He said, "Burglar alarm must be busted."

Ray bent over his cue stick and made his shot, sending the cue ball into the number-six ball, which hit the two ball into the side pocket. He then followed Matthew and Craig to where Bobby was moping.

Craig asked him what happened and Bobby said, "Joyce kicked me out. Actually, she had her new boyfriend do the honors. He's white."

Ray said, "Uh, don't mean to burst your bubble, kid, but so are you."

"I ain't white. I was born in South Africa."

Ray stared at Bobby's head, frowning a little, like he was curious.

"Yep, something's definitely gone loose in there."

Craig said to Bobby, "Shit, man, you let a white guy beat on you?" He saw Ray giving him a look, an expression of incredulity, and said, "What?"

"You've been around me for so long you forgot which side you're rooting for."

Matthew said, "Time you got yourself cleaned up, young blood," and handed Bobby a cold one. Bobby drank the beer telling Matthew he took a shower this morning. "I mean you need to clean up your act—get off drugs and get a job."

"I know that's what you want me to do. But you know, I can't say the same for me."

Ray picked out a drugstore lighter from Bobby's Afro. "There's my lighter."

Bobby looked toward the doorway. "How long's the butler been standing there?"

Matthew said, "Hey, Nood."

"Carter is here, sir," the butler said, "and he's brought the en-*tou*-rage."

"Thanks, Nood. Tell 'em I'll be right down."

Craig gulped down the rest of his beer, put the empty on the coffee table and said, "Okay, Ray, you ready to go?" Putting on his shoes.

"Yeah," Ray said.

Bobby asked where they were going. Craig said they were going to the funeral of an old college buddy of theirs, Al Wooley. Bobby asked what happened to him. Craig said, "He died." Ray explained that Al Wooley was flying when his plane crashed into swampland. Realizing the tragedy he reminded Craig, "And you know, we almost went with him?"

Craig said, "Jesus Christ, how lucky are we?"

"Fucking lucky."

They said no more. Craig and Ray stood there, both lost in their thoughts.

Matthew brought them back. "So, Al Wooley …"

Ray said, "Yes, what a tragedy," shaking his head to show some respect. "Gonna miss that bastard."

Craig said, "We better go if we want to see the mashed-up body before they close the casket."

"We wouldn't want to miss that."

They hurried out and the butler reappeared. Matthew, knowing it was coming, raised his eyebrows expectantly.

"Carter is here, sir. With the en-*tou*-rage."

"I have to go," Matthew said to Bobby, "otherwise he's going to keep doing that."

Bobby was alone in the man cave, watching Matthew's fight on the plasma TV. He heard Joyce calling from the hall, "Bobby?"

He didn't move. "You getting warmer."

"I came to see that there were no hard feelings—"

She emerged in the doorway and found him, the sight of him stopping her in her tracks, whatever she wanted to say now gone.

"Oh my God."

"I know. My eyes don't usually pop out this much."

"What happened to you?"

"Your new boyfriend didn't give you the four-one-one?"

That got her moving, kneeling in front of him on the couch and then folding her handbag and placing it on the floor, not far from her.

"Chris did this to you?"

"He did this and then some."

"He told me there were no fights," Joyce said, hurt, her eyes cast down. "He lied to me."

"He lied to me too. He told me he was delivering a check."

Joyce looked up at him, making a face with sad eyes. "Why would Chris be delivering you a check?"

"Hey, I don't question a guy who says he's delivering a check."

The funeral was short, and was soon over, everyone was leaving the chapel. Craig looked at Al Wooley in the open casket. Ray had his tablet, watching and listening to Matthew's fight on earphones.

"He looks like he's sleeping," Craig said.

"Matt's survived through four*teen* rounds so far." Ray looked at Al in the casket and said, "And when he's asleep, he looks like he's dead."

"You know, I can't see myself in a casket."

"I see you in a casket."

Craig turned from the casket to see Ray with his tablet. "You do?"

"Every night I go to sleep."

Craig left Al Wooley in the casket and came down the altar. "Jesus Christ, you dream of seeing me in a casket?"

"Oh, it's no dream."

They were leaving when, over the earphones of the tablet, a boxing commentator's voice bellowed, "Holy hell!"

Ray said, "What happened?"

"*Ho-o-oly hell!*" the boxing commentator screamed in Ray's earphones.

"*What happened?*"

One of the pallbearers looked around, made sure that the chapel was empty, before waking Al Wooley. "Get up, Al. They're gone."

Al Wooley sat up in a dark suit and pale makeup, alive. He said, "My God, this casket is so comfortable—I was kind of getting used to it. Scary thing to think about." He said, "All right," climbing out. "Close it. Make sure it's locked up tight."

They became aware of footsteps.

"Someone's coming," the pallbearer said.

Al Wooley ran out a back door.

Matthew Piars, still in his boxing gloves with the matching shorts, boots and robe, the hood over his head, sat on the bench in his dressing room. He looked dazed. His cornermen were with him, in shirts with *Team Piars* embroidered on the back. They gave the Champ some time to let what happened sink in. It was his trainer who finally broke the silence.

"You okay, Champ?"

"Leave me alone for a while, alright?"

"It wasn't your fault McGinnis dropped in the ring."

Matthew turned his head and stared at Carter before he said, "Not my fault? Carter, I hit him, and his neck fucking snapped. *Jesus*."

"Look on the bright side."

"There's a bright side to a fighter dying in the ring?"

Carter said, "Sure," shrugged, over confident. "There's a bright side to everything." Matthew kept staring at him and Carter wasn't sure of himself anymore. "Isn't there?"

"Your mother breastfed you too long." Matthew dismissed the cornermen, saying, "Give me privacy."

They filed out, Carter hanging back as he remembered something else, then turning to the champ in his robe. Carter cleared his throat to say Bobby called. "Been calling since the fluke. He wants to know who won the fight."

"I bet he's confused out of his stoned mind."

"And also, your wifey called. I told her you didn't want to talk to anybody." Carter grinned. "She said she'll call me back when I have something she'd want to hear."

"Millicent calls, give me the phone," Matthew said. "Bobby calls, tell him it's his own damn fault for betting his last dollar on the fight—and against his own brother."

Matthew was left alone. He allowed the silence to ride his emotions. The quieter it got, though, the better he heard that snap—Jesus, the sound of McGinnis's neck breaking as he delivered an uppercut to the underside of his chin that ended the man's career and his life. Then watching the referee count to ten and expecting McGinnis to get up. First time in Matthew's fighting career he wanted his opponent to beat the count, show some fucking life. Matthew standing there scared, his heart racing, and when the referee finished his count and McGinnis was still down, Matthew knew, God Almighty, he had killed a man in the ring. The last round kept replaying in his head again and again. He tried to block it from his mind, but it was hopeless. Matthew wanted his wife, the only person he could talk to when times got bad, somebody to hold him and tell him everything would be okay, you know, somebody who was on his side. She was almost always on his mind.

Movement in the dressing room. Not from Matthew, from someone else. Coming from the next room, the bathroom. Dark in there.

"Goddammit—I said, I want to be left alone."

The noise stopped.

Matthew looked around and then rose from the bench. Jagger emerged from the bathroom in his green scrubs like an apparition out of the night.

They stared at each other for a long, intense moment.

Jagger said, "Mattie."

Matthew looking at Jagger but not knowing shit who he was looking at.

Matthew showed him a frown. "My sister used to call me that."

Jagger surprised him saying, "Heard she was taken. Kidnapped and then for her body to wash up on the beach. Damn." Knowing only what the people close to Matthew knew.

Maybe he was a stalker, Matthew told himself, and if so call security and have the motherfucker thrown out.

But Matthew hesitated. He was curious and said, "Who are you?"

Jagger apologized in Afrikaans, "*Jammer . . .*" and Matthew translated it in English, *sorry*, in his head. "I don't speak the tongue of your foster father, I speak the tongue of your biological father."

An accent to go with the redheaded negro look.

Matthew said, "Nobody called me Mattie except my sister and my best friend from my childhood, Jagger Zuma."

There was Jagger's smile again. It brightened his whole features, made him recognizable.

"Mattie-*ee*."

Matthew said, "Jagger!" his voice rising, delighted. "Jesus Christ!"

The prisoner and the boxer hugged each other, glad for this reunion.

"Son of a bitch."

Jagger said, "Yes, she was a bitch."

"Wait. Is this really Jagger? Jagger Zuma? The wimp I hung out wit' in South Africa?"

"That's me."

"Jesus Christ. Jagger, look at you."

"Look at me."

"It's great to see you."

They hugged again and then pulled back, smiling at each other.

Matthew said, "Where the fuck have you been hiding? Last I heard, your dad left you in the woods. The whole village went in there to look for you, but we never found you. We had to accept the inevitable that you may have been anaconda food."

"I came back."

"You survived in the woods on your own for twen-*ty* years?"

Jagger hesitated. "So much I have to tell you."

Matthew looked at Jagger's fire engine red hair. "Damn, Jagger, what's wit' the red dye?"

Jagger said, "I have red hair?" Putting it on.

Look at that, grinning at him.

"How'd you make it out of South Africa?"

"I snuck on a garbage ship leaving for America." He paused, his eyes on Matthew before saying, "So the whole village looked for me, huh?"

"Yeah," Matthew said. "My dad and the entire police department put up a search party."

"How did they know my mom and dad abandoned me in the forest?"

Jagger watched Matthew stare at him for a moment and then sit on the bench again, brush the hood of his robe from his head and say, "I saw your old man take you."

"You saw?"

Matthew nodded. "I waited hours. Then I watched him come out. Without you."

Jagger seemed to think about it before saying, "Good you stayed out. The forest is no place for a seven-year-old."

"I couldn't believe your parents did that to you."

"They chose the easy way out of poverty. Get rid of the suckling, less mouths to feed."

Matthew's heart sank.

Jagger said, "Don't cry for me, *vriend*. I survived. I'm here, aren't I?"

Matthew nodded, accepting it. "You're here."

"I'm grateful to your old man for putting up the search party. Man was a damn good cop."

"Apparently not good enough to keep his life."

Jagger raised his eyebrows. "Croaked?"

"Sniper picked him off a golf course."

"Damn."

"Damn is right."

Jagger paused, but then went on, "And what about Mommy Dearest?"

Matthew dithered over a question that was supposed to be simple. "Still living," he said. "I took off after finding Izzy's body on the beach, stayed away for a year. It was finding her like that broke me. Bobby sent word our dad got shot. So I went back home to Africa for the funeral. I arrived too late. Bobby had already left. My mom said he'd gone looking for me when it looked like I wasn't coming home for the funeral."

"I'd love to know how the idiot got into America."

"They were transporting this guy who'd died on vacation. Bobby took the corpse out of the body bag and hid in its place."

Jagger was smiling again. "When desperate times call for desperate measures, the kid can be resourceful."

Matthew dropped his head in a chuckle. Then looked up when Jagger asked, "And you?"

"This criminal court judge fostered me. Vincent Gray Murphy. Man flew me to America wit' him."

"You lucky bastard," Jagger said, but was smiling. He took time to look at his friend, noticed the wedding ring on Matthew's finger as he peeled off the boxing gloves. "So there's actually a Mrs. Matthew Piars?"

Yes, for over two years now, Matthew remembering his wedding. He had stood at the altar, facing his bride. Millicent, a beautiful young Hawaiian brunette in a flowing white gown and veil. The minister had delivered those seven words that changed his life forever. "I now pronounce you husband and wife." The minister between them saying, "You may kiss the bride." Family and friends watched as Matthew took his bride in his arms and gave her a deep, lingering kiss that promised her his heart and soul. The church erupted with cheers and applause. Matthew had waved his hand at them in dismissal, which got laughs. Matthew looking up and saying, deadpan, "No, I mean it, get outta 'ere." Getting more laughs as he again kissed his bride.

Jagger smiled, very happy for him.

"I'm also a Dad," Matthew said.

"Shut your mouth. You mean to tell me there's another one of you roaming the earth? How long did you court Millicent before knocking her up?"

"Two months."

"Wow. You didn't waste any time, did you?"

Jagger didn't smile. Still, Matthew knew he was kidding. What Jagger was saying was he was a horny bastard. Matthew smiled.

Smiled and let it fade as he looked at Jagger, really looked at him, coming to grips with the situation for the first time since they reunited, Matthew saying, "You're standing." Astonished.

"I've been healed."

Matthew looked completely nonplussed. He said, "I didn't think there was a cure for cerebral palsy."

Matthew appraised Jagger in his prison scrubs.

"Dude, what's wit' the scrubs? Got put on community service?"

"Nope," Jagger said. "Got done the Harrison Ford way."

"You were falsely accused of murder?"

"No, I did it."

"What did you do, Jagger?"

"Nothing major ... Butchered my mom."

"Jesus Christ. You came to America to kill your mom?"

Jagger didn't care for the accusation. "She came to America to get away from what she'd done there—leaving her only child for dead in the woods. But I got her, in eight chunks. If you count her baby feeders. Which I got nothing out of."

"Jagger ..."

Giving him a look of disappointment.

"The bitch deserved it, Matt. Every blow."

"And your dad? I mean you didn't ...?"

"Haven't found the jackass. But I will. You can count on it. Until then, all's good."

"You bust out of stir."

"I'm collecting supplies. I work the contraband in the prison."

It caused Matthew to pause, looking at Jagger to catch on to what he meant.

"Contraband?"

Jagger started to tell him yeah, it's when one guy …

"I know what contraband is, *jou naai*," Matthew hissed. "What I meant was, who the fuck appointed you the contraband guy?"

"Well, there was twenty of us. I picked the bigger rock."

Matthew paused again.

"Twenty inmates wit' twenty rocks, and you picked the bigger rock?"

"That's right."

"Damn. How big was your rock?"

Jagger held his hands apart in front of him. He said, "This big."

"Jesus Christ. Jagger, if you had the bigger rock, you shouldn't be running the contraband. It ought to be the guy wit' the smallest rock. They bamboozled you, *vriend*."

It took Jagger awhile to say, "I believe they did."

Matthew shook his head now. "Jesus. Jagger, you have to go back to prison."

Jagger waited. "I'm sorry, I didn't quite hear what you said."

"Go *back*."

"Go back? But I haven't been to the strip club yet."

"We'll talk more later …" Matthew smiled and had to admit, it was good to see his friend again. "Now that I know where you are." He said, "Wait. What prison have they got you locked up?"

"Sing Sing."

"Jesus. The Americans make even prison sound like a musical." Matthew was looking toward the dressing room door, ensuring that it was closed, before he said, "Alright," like he was starting over. "Go back."

"Fine, I'll go back to prison," Jagger said. He went in the bathroom and came out again with a metal bedpan. "An inmate asked for this. You're not using it, you mind if I take it?"

"No, I might use it."

"Why do you need a bedpan? There's a toilet bowl right in the next room."

"Jagger, for God's sake, go back to prison."

Jagger wasted no more time, he darted into the bathroom with the bedpan. Matthew moved to the doorway and looked in. Jagger was nowhere to be seen. He located the air vent, way up on the grim, gritty tiled wall. Other than the door, the vent was the only means of escape, though it was too small for a man of Jagger's size.

Joyce asked him to come back home and then fixed him something to eat, catering to his every whim, Joyce telling him she was sorry and if she could take it back, she would. Every time she put a plate in front of him, she'd touch his face and ask, "How're you feeling?"

Bobby said, "Sore," made his voice weak to sound pathetic. "But this beef Stroganoff with rice helps me deal with the pain." He scooped rice into his mouth. "Keep it coming, chef."

"Okay."

Joyce got up from the table and went to the stove to serve him a third plate.

She said, "Look, Bobby, I'm sorry about Chris. He didn't have to do that to you." Joyce paused in her serving and smiled. "Although I'm flattered he fought for my honor."

Bobby felt that he was losing his girlfriend's respect, so he feigned a cry of pain. "My eyes! My eyes!"

Hurrying over with his third plate of beef and rice Joyce said, "Oh, you poor baby." She set the plate down on the table, Bobby still working on his second. She tended to him, took his swollen face in her hands and softly kissed him on each eye. "How's that?"

"A lot better, thanks."

She sat down and said, "And don't worry about Chris. We won't be seeing him around here anymore."

Hope gleamed in Bobby's eyes. "Ever?"

"Ever."

"That's good, 'cause Chris was mean."

"It's a good thing I found that out before I had his baby."

Bobby was chewing. He swallowed and said, "You know, Joyce," going into his pathetic mode, "knowing Chris ain't ever coming back will heal me faster."

Joyce smiled, pleased.

"More beer?"

"If you blow me, do I not cum?"

They were cuddled up on the sofa, watching *Oprah* together. Joyce asked him if he wanted to watch something else. Bobby insisted he was fine with *Oprah*. "She's the man." Joyce said really, they could watch what he wanted to watch, it was fine. Bobby said aight, took the remote from her and flipped it to porn.

"You wanna watch porn?"

Bobby wiggled a tooth with his fingers saying, "I think your boyfriend chipped my tooth."

"Porn it is."

There was a moment of sex sounds coming from the TV, and then there was hard pounding on the trailer door.

"That's a real boner killer," Bobby said, "I'll get it," pushing up from the sofa.

Joyce looked alarmed. "It could be Chris."

Bobby doubted it. Then withdrew cowardly, asking her, "You made it clear to Chris it was over between you two, right?"

Uh-huh.

Good. Bobby opened the door. He looked in the trailer at Joyce curled in the sofa.

"It's Craig."

Joyce said, "Hey, Craig!"

Didn't get an answer. Bobby stepped out of the trailer, closed the door behind him, and turned to the weightlifter there, who wasn't Craig.

"Hey," Bobby said.

"Time to pay up."

Bobby dug in his pants pocket and produced a wad of currency. The weightlifter swiped it out of his hand and counted it. Then stopped, giving Bobby a contemptuous look.

"You're ten dollars short."

"We agreed thirty'd be the price."

The weightlifter pointed as he said, "Ten for each black eye, ten for the broken tooth, and another ten for the busted nose. Forty."

Bobby knew better than to argue with the guy he had hired to beat him up. Resigned, he gave up the extra ten.

"Thanks again."

"Always a pleasure pounding on a dingbat."

He walked away and Bobby went back in the trailer.

Tasso walked up to the blind young man, who was sitting alone on the bench in the shamrock golf shirt, and said, "Hi there."

The blind young man turned his head to Tasso's voice. "Hello, voice that I don't know."

"They call me Tasso."

"Hi, Tasso. They call me Shaquille."

"Hi, Shaquille. Might I ask what you're doing on the bench?"

"You mean beside sitting? Waiting for the bus."

"I'm afraid your bus ain't coming, Shaq."

"How come?"

"I mean you're stuck on that bench. Yep, you're going to be waiting for that bus of yours for a very long time, Shaq. No way a bus is coming through these parts."

"Why not?"

"Because no carriage has come through since the cemetery opened back in 1736. Sonny, you've been sitting on a boneyard bench."

"Hmm. I must've taken a wrong turn somewhere."

Tasso, in soiled coveralls and a worn-out snapback cap, said to the blind young man, "Thought you were one of 'em kids come looking for will-o'-the-wisp. Yep, for a while now kids have been breaking into the boneyard hunting for the foolish fire. The cemetery is not a playground, young man. There are unexplained things living in the cemetery. They can attach themselves to you. You know? You don't take care, you never know what may follow you home." He paused and said, "Need assistance to the bus stop?"

"I'm smart and capable enough to know where the bus stop is." With a different tone, sounding like a young blind man who believes he's been disrespected, boasting now, saying, "Last year I almost got into college. *Smart.*"

"Impressive."

"Eh?"

Tasso said, "I can see, and I never got past the campus gates."

Al Wooley walked up the carpeted hallway to his hotel room, he'd managed to get away from his own funeral without being detected. And soon as his life insurance money kicked in he'd fly off to Barbados.

Al unlocked the door, and stepped inside. He took off his suit coat, draped it over a chair, made himself a drink from the minibar, picked up the phone, and dialed the cemetery groundskeeper, telling him, "Tasso? I'm at the hotel. Bury the casket."

He hung up the phone and took his drink on the balcony. Weather was changing, the air a little cooler. Dusk was coming. Al set his glass on the rail and lit a cigarette while looking at the view of Manhattan. Lights were coming on in the buildings like stars coming out. He got the butt sparked up and blew smoke into the breeze.

He leaned against the railing. It let go and Al Wooley fell forward with it, screaming.

Ninety feet below, Ray and Craig were seated at a café terrace finishing their coffee. "Can you believe Matt actually killed another fighter in the ring on national TV," Craig said, "and got to walk?"

"I know," Ray said. "It's reassuring to know that if I ever want to get away with murder, I could just do it in the boxing ring, on national TV, in front of thousands of people, and I won't go to jail."

Craig took the conversation to another level, asking, "How many people do you reckon get to go to heaven?"

"I was afraid this talk of Matt killing in the boxing ring would bring up the topic of heaven. And the answer to your question is, none of them. You die, you rot. And that's the end of it."

Ray sipped his coffee.

"Don't you like to take comfort in the thought of your wife in heaven, looking down on you?"

"God, no."

"Why not?"

"Because the very thought of my dead wife watching my every move frightens the shit out of me."

Craig said, "And you frighten me."

Then Al Wooley landed *smack* on their table, throwing them back.

"Jesus Christ."

Ray said, "Daaamn." He looked into the dead guy's face. "Craig, it's Al."

The maintenance guy knocked on the door of Al Wooley's hotel room. He said, "Hotel maintenance. I'm here to fix the balcony railing."

No answer.

He knocked again.

"Hello?"

The hotel maintenance guy let himself in the room with a master key.

There was nobody in the room. He looked toward the balcony, frowning. Something about it didn't look right. Stepping out onto the balcony he saw why. The railing was gone. He moved to the edge and looked down at Al Wooley's body, ninety feet below, splattered down there in the street. "Goddamn it. There goes my pension."

"Did he just fall out of the sky?"

Craig looking at Al Wooley's dead body as he said it and heard Ray's surprised voice say, "Imagine that, man fell right out of the sky."

Craig looking up at the sky now. "He must've pissed God off for the last time."

Ray said, "Got himself booted out of heaven."

Dusk had settled.

Jagger was heading back to Sing Sing. He cut through the residential area of Lafayette Avenue.

He saw high beams coming at him, headlights and the wailing sirens of law enforcement on the quiet street. Several

NYPD cars blew past and Jagger dove behind some stairs and the NYPD cars continued down the street.

Jagger came out of the stairs onto the sidewalk and watched the taillights until they disappeared, the NYPD cars turning off into a side road.

Someone was watching him.

Behind him.

He wheeled around. An ordinary-looking, freckled-face girl in her early teens stood on the stoop of her house. She stared wide-eyed at the redheaded black man in the green prison scrubs. She held an oven tray of chicken pot pie pockets in her oven-mitted hands.

Jagger held his palms out to show he was harmless. "Don't be alarmed. I'm not as dangerous as the hair makes me look. I can explain." He paused and quickly thought up an explanation for his strange appearance. "Community service."

She relaxed, a little. "Why did you duck into the stairs?"

"Reflex."

The girl moved down the steps to the garbage can with her chicken pot pie pockets.

Jagger said, "What have you got there, food?"

"It's my mom and dad's anniversary, and I wanted to do something special for them, so I cooked dinner." She said, "I lost my jewelry in one of the chicken pot pie pockets."

"Oh, no."

"Oh, yes." She sat on the stoop with her ruined pot pie pockets. "I ruined my parents' anniversary dinner."

She was looking at him now, studying him.

"Why do you glow?"

Jagger said, "It's the soap." She didn't know what he was talking about.

The prisoner moved toward her on the stoop, though keeping a safe companionable distance between them, not wanting to upset her any more than she was. He stooped over and regarded the dozen pot pie pockets.

"Your charm bracelet is inside"—the Redheaded Negro pointing—"this pocket."

The teenage girl slipped off her oven mitts and picked up the pie pocket he'd singled out and broke it in half, careful as it was still hot from the oven. Her silver charm bracelet dangled out of the torn pie pocket.

She said, "There it is!"

And he echoed, "There it is."

"Thank you so much."

"No sweat."

Getting up, she ascended the stoop to the doormat and right away turned. "How did you know it was my charm bracelet?"

The sidewalk was empty. Jagger was gone.

Matthew sat at a table in one of Sing Sing's private visiting rooms, watching through bulletproof glass as a guard brought Jagger out in handcuffs. The guard unlocked Jagger and he took the chair opposite him.

Matthew said, "Hey."

Jagger said, "Hey."

They stared silently at each other through the glass, smiling, two old friends—best friends—who hadn't seen each other in years, happy to be reunited once again.

"*Hoe gaan dit?*" Matthew said.

"I'm good," Jagger said. "You haven't forgotten your father's tongue. I'm glad."

"How long have you been in this sardine can?"

"I have completed four years. Got a hundred more to go."

"A hundred?"

Jagger slowly nodded his head up and down. He said, "Yep, yep, yep." And said, "The number isn't so big till you're pissing and shitting and sleeping in the same room you live in."

"Listen, Jagger? Whatever you want, know that I'm there for you. Anything you need, man—protection, cigarettes, hard cash ... duct tape to tape your asshole shut."

Jagger grinning now. "I appreciate the gesture."

"Anything for an old friend." Matthew waited as long as he could, almost a minute, and said, "Something I want to ask you."

"If it's about the bedpan, let me tell you—you do not want it back."

"This is a favor."

"You want me to shank somebody?"

"No—"

"'Cause I don't mind."

"Just listen …" Matthew paused and gave Jagger a serious look now. "My kid doesn't have a godfather yet. Now I've talked it over wit' Millicent, and she knows how much it'd mean to me if, well, you could be our baby's godfather."

"Damn, Matt," Jagger said, and smiled, deeply moved. "Don't make me cry. You know what they do to inmates who cry?"

"No, what?"

Jagger shrugged. "I don't know. I never cried." He smiled and said, "Champ, I'd be honored to be the little nose-digger's godfather—shit."

Matthew sat back in his chair, a happy man. "Oh, man, that's just great. You've made me and the missus very happy. I'd kiss you if this glass wasn't in my way."

Jagger said, "Good thing it is. Wouldn't want to give the guards the wrong impression."

He jokingly blew Matthew a kiss. The two men laughed heartily.

A GUIDING LIGHT

One year later, March eleventh. Fresh out of bed at nine to ten on a Monday morning, Matthew, in gray sweatpants and white undershirt over his masculine frame, stood at the kitchen counter scratching himself and saying, "What's left for a retired boxer to do?" He saw the fresh brewed coffee the butler had made. "Drink coffee." He poured himself a cup and paused before taking a sip. Matthew said, "Now I forget. Do I brush my teeth before or after breakfast?" He shrugged and drank the coffee black and bitter, the way he was used to.

The linoleum floor was cool beneath his bare feet. Matthew's eyes went to the neglected moving boxes around the house, all marked *Millicent's Kitchen Stuff*, a grim reminder that his marriage was now over, losing the love of his life to his best man. Three years of bliss down the toilet. He raised the cup to the boxes and said, "Here's to single life again at thirty-four. Man, I didn't think I'd be back where I started."

Don't get mad. Take your life day by day, Matthew thinking it as Bobby walked in in a dark hoodie and carrying some kid's Harry Potter backpack, his eyes bloodshot. The boy was stoned out of his mind.

"Hey, bro," Bobby said, and then saw the moving boxes. "Millicent move out?"

"Yes, and her stuff will catch up wit' her later." Matthew poured himself another cup of coffee, unhurried. "So, young blood … what are you doing here, cutting so early into my morning?"

"I got a problem."

Matthew looked at Bobby, always coming to him with problems. "Alright, young blood, what trouble are you in now? I mean that I can make go away wit' bribery."

"This time it ain't Justin Bieber."

Matthew waited.

Bobby said, "This trouble has four legs and a tail."

Matthew was patient with his junkie brother, his blood and, God help him, his child's uncle.

"Say what?"

Bobby turned his back to him. Matthew was looking at a smooth coated Jack Russell Terrier that was clinging stubbornly to the Harry Potter backpack. The dog was growling like an engine.

"That's not my dog. Whose dog is that?"

"I don't know!" Bobby said. "I can't shake him loose!" He backed up toward Matthew in hysteria. "Get him off my backpack!"

Matthew said, "Alright, alright," still unhurried. He set his coffee down on the kitchen island. "God, it's way too early for this."

He faced the Jack Russell clinging to the backpack he knew was stolen. Matthew took hold of the dog with one hand and, using his free hand, pinched the dog's muzzle and loosened its grip on the backpack. He put the dog on the linoleum floor. Right away, it jumped up and clung onto the backpack.

Bobby shrieked.

Matthew said, "Hang on." He loosened the dog's hold, and it bounded from his arms back to the backpack. "Why does it keep going to the backpack?"

"I don't know." Playing dumb. He was very good at that.

Bobby started to shake his body, dementedly, desperate to be rid of the goddamn dog. The dog only swung back and forth. The idiot got so into the project of shaking off the dog that he began dancing and singing to Odyssey's *Use It Up and Wear It Out.*

"One, two, three, shake your body down. One, two, three, shake your body down to me. Shake it down to me."

"Alright, Disco Queen," Matthew said, fed up with this whole shenanigan. He removed the dog from the backpack.

This time he held onto the dog tightly. "Alright, what's in the backpack, young blood?"

Bobby looked at Matthew and raised his eyebrows, looking as innocent as possible.

"Nothing."

"What do you have in the backpack?"

Bobby said, "Marijuana," and gasped, astonished. "You think *that's* what he's after?"

"I would say . . . *no.*"

Matthew beckoned with his free hand for the bag, and Bobby drew away saying no way. "Get your own Harry Potter bag." Matthew telling him to hand over the fucking bag. He grabbed at the top of the backpack and held on to it, didn't show any sign of letting go till finally Bobby surrendered it over, saying, "Aight, aight, you want it? Shit, take it. It's yours, aight?"

Matthew set the dog on the floor, at his feet, and pointed a stern finger at it. "*Stay.*"

He unzipped the backpack, looked inside and felt his stomach tighten and anger rise in him. He had to stay calm to keep his cool. He'd find out what was going on, do that first, before he thought to grab Bobby's head and put it through the fucking wall.

Matthew reached in the backpack. He took out a good-sized steak, cooked, dripping with grease, and asked Bobby, "Whose steak is this?"

The Jack Russell barked, twice, as if saying, "Mine!"

Matthew said, "Is that true, young blood? Is it the dog's steak?"

Bobby dropped his eyes, chagrined. "Yeah."

Matthew thought of hitting him.

"You took this steak?"

"I had the munchies."

Like that made it all right.

"Young blood, you stole food from a *dog*?"

"Not intentionally."

Punch him right in his scraggly teeth.

Matthew said, "How do you *un*intentionally steal steak from a dog?"

"When you close your eyes and take it."

Matthew sighed and let the matter go. He gave the Jack Russell Terrier back the steak. Now that it had what it'd been after, the dog trotted happily out of the mansion with the steak in its mouth.

Bobby yelled after the dog, "I hope you choke on it!"

Iggy stood with his face pressed between the iron bars of his cell. He said, "Hey, Jagger!" his voice carrying through the wide prison corridor.

"What?"

Jagger was also at the bars of his own cell.

Iggy said, "How great is this, man? The toilet and bed in one room!"

Jagger said, "Who needs diapers?"

"I hear you, man."

Matthew, Craig and Ray were on the couch watching Matthew's last fight. The boxing commentator, back then, had screamed, saying, "Holy hell! Ho-o-oly hell! He's down! McGinnis is *dooown*!"

Ray said, "That commentator screams any louder, he's gonna shit himself."

"If only Thomas McGinnis had known he was going to die in the ring that night," Craig said, "he could've forfeited the fight."

"It's why I call in sick for work whenever I feel a cold coming on. You know? It could be God saying, 'You're outta here, Ray.'"

Matthew wasn't into it. "We've watched this fight a thousand times."

"Yes," Craig said, "but we haven't watched it a thousand and *one* times."

Matthew looked at him incredulously. "The death of a boxer is entertaining to you?"

It was Ray who answered. "Sure it is. They wouldn't put it on national TV if it wasn't."

"That's one moment of my career I'm not proud of." Matthew saw that the remote was right next to him. He said, "Right, and I *can* turn it off." Flicked the fucker off.

Craig sat back in the big couch. "Getting your head snapped off your fucking neck's got to be the worst way to go. Now, had he gotten chewed by a rabid pit bull …"

Bobby came in shivering from the cold. He said, "Brrr! It's colder than a witch's tit out there."

Craig said to Ray. "How cold is a witch's tit?"

"Slightly warmer than the balls on a brass monkey, one would hope."

Bobby flung his backpack onto the floor. Craig and Ray looked at each other, and then started kicking and stomping the backpack. Matthew took it from there; he stepped in, picked it up, and disposed of it in the trash.

Bobby reacted to that. "Hey! Come on, bro! That's my Harry Potter backpack."

"Oh, I'm sorry. When you tossed it like that, I assumed you didn't want it."

Craig said, "Yeah, Bob."

"Bobby," Ray said, "you're a twenty-six year old man and you're carrying around a Harry Potter backpack?"

"Well, the kid I stole it from idolized Harry Potter."

"You know," Ray said, "every time you speak, your idiot temperature rises."

Craig asked Bobby, what's the matter.

"Joyce and I had a huge fight," Bobby said. "She kicked me out of the trailer, and now I'm bunking with Z, whose brother is his bookie. I mean, talk about a dysfunctional family."

Ray shook his head, smiling, saying, "Only a fight with a woman can make a man look that damn pathetic."

Matthew, changing the subject, said, "Listen, you guys? If it's all the same to you, I'm going to skip the strip club tonight. I just want to stay home and spend a quiet evening alone."

Craig wouldn't have it. He said, "Come on, big guy, you just got divorced. You've finally got your foot off the land mine. You're free to invade other territories."

"I need to be wit' Danny, you know, go through this hard time wit' my child."

Ray gasped dramatically, thinking he had Matthew all figured out. "He's going down and he's taking the kid with him!"

"It's okay wit' me if you all don't want to be here."

Bobby sagged on the couch. "Oh good, 'cause I was getting tired of pretending."

"I'm sure you all have other plans."

Ray looked depressed. "I don't have plans."

Matthew said, "How come?"

"Well, because I've misplaced my date book, and I hadn't memorized my schedule for the week. Plus Shelly dumped me."

Might as well get that out of the way.

Bobby said, "What?"

Thinking Bobby hadn't heard him Ray repeated, "Shelly *dumped* me." He said, "I finally find a good woman to cater to me, and she hightails it out of the Village."

Matthew said, "How did Shelly get out of the kitchen? Was the gate around it unlocked?"

"Apparently somebody blabbed that her cooking was the only reason I put up with her."

Bobby, the one who'd blabbed, said, "I think I better leave," and rushed out of there.

Ray, catching on, scowled at him as he went out the door.

Bobby had lined cocaine on the coffee table. As he bent over to snort, Matthew grabbed the back of his neck and squeezed hard until Bobby was off the couch and on the floor, on his knees, screaming in pain—"Aah! Aaah!"

"The fuck are you doing?"

Bobby brushed the cocaine off the table with the sleeve of his sweatshirt. "I was … I was wiping the dandruff off the table, that's all."

Matthew knew his brother was dumb, but not that dumb. He released his hold and the butler walked in to offer him a bottle of beer, wet, and ice cold, on a silver platter.

"Your beer, Mr. Piars."

"Thank you, Nood." Matthew held up the beer. The butler produced a bottle opener and removed the metal cap. Matthew took a sip.

Seeing that the butler was about to leave, Bobby said, "Where's my beer?"

The butler brought another bottle from his tailcoat. "I was saving this ..." He tossed the bottle to Bobby and walked out.

Bobby held the beer out in front of him in disgust. "Blech. This beer's all warm." He pried the cap off with his teeth. "You know, bro, I don't trust that butler."

"Now why do you say that?"

"Man pulled a beer out his tailcoat. I seen Clint Eastwood do that, except Clint didn't pull a beer."

Matthew nodded. He'd seen the movie too. It was a good one.

The telephone rang.

Matthew said, "If that's Murphy, tell him I'm not in."

"Aight, but that leaves nothing else for us to talk about." Bobby picked up the phone and said, "Speak." He listened and said, "Yeah, this is Mr. Piars." He listened again and said, "Jesus. I'll be sure to tell Mr. Piars."

He hung up, and sipped his beer, Matthew looking at him.

"Who was that?"

Bobby said, "Oh. That was Danny's day care."

Nothing important.

"Everything okay?" Matthew sipped his beer.

"Well, according to the po*lice*man who called?" Matthew's face was a mask of panic. "Danny beat up on some kid. Right now they're waiting for the kid to come out of the emergency room so they can get his side of the story."

But he got no response. Matthew had left.

And Bobby was off the couch, lickety-split, and down on all fours on the rug. "Still good, still good," he said, and inhaled cocaine off the rug and closed his eyes in ecstasy. "Lord, take me now."

The rest stop on I-87 was vacant.

Bobby would've waited until he got to Z's apartment if he hadn't needed to go bad. He approached the middle stall and stopped to give the door a slight nudge with the toe of his sneaker. The door opened like a slow, unhinged jaw.

Bobby said, feeling uneasy about this, "I have *got* to get over my fear of public bathrooms."

He tentatively stepped into the stall and uncovered a large plastic bag of cocaine bulging from the toilet bowl.

"Fear gone," Bobby said in a singsong tone.

Matthew waited in the driver's seat of the Jaguar, his left hand on the top arc of the steering wheel, thumbing his wedding ring. He was wondering if he'd given up on his marriage too soon or overreacted. Had his marriage been strong enough that it could have been salvaged? He'd found out that his wife had been screwing his best man for sixteen months. *Sixteen months*—Jesus Christ. Could he have forgiven her, let bygones be bygones, and moved on? Could anyone?

God, everything was so messed up. Why hadn't he seen it? He was so madly in love he probably wouldn't have assigned any significance to his doubts if she hadn't come to him, crying she'd lost her wedding ring. He'd then found the ring in the bathroom at Darryl's house. Matthew had stared at his wife's missing ring in the toothbrush cup by Darryl's sink and wanted to punch his lights out. He blamed himself for being a fool and actually believing she loved him. Night after night of mad, passionate lovemaking, meanwhile unaware that the woman who shared his bed was fucking around. The rational part of his mind reminded him that she was a young woman, eleven years his junior. She had some fun left in her. They got married too soon.

Perhaps it wasn't too late to save their love.

Bobby exited the rest stop, his arms wrapped around his stomach, a bulge under his shirt—the kilo of coke from the toilet bowl. He slid into the passenger seat and closed the door.

"Sorry it took me so long in there," Bobby said. "My zipper got caught on something very valuable to me."

Matthew glared at him, not saying anything—he knew.

"What?" Bobby said.

Matthew continued to glare at him —

"What?"

—and glared some more.

"Oh, all *right*, I'll go wash my hands."

Bobby got out of the Jaguar.

Minutes after their departure, a black Mercedes pulled in at the rest stop. Out of the backseat, a one-armed black man in his mid-thirties held a white guy, about the same age and thirty pounds lighter, at gunpoint.

The white guy had undercover police officer written all over him.

He led the one-armed black guy into the restroom.

The apartment was trashed, and Z was clearing up. Bobby rushed in, hunched over and holding his stomach, saying, "Hey, Z."

"Your half of the rent is due tonight."

That stopped Bobby, on his way to the bathroom.

"The other day, you said I could live here rent free."

Yes, Z did say that. Those were the good old days. "I was so young and so stupid."

"You want the rent tonight?"

"Not me, my bookie."

"He was here?"

Z nodded, putting the apartment back together. "Told me if he came by tonight and I didn't have his money, he'd do this to my face," Z said, holding up the broken pieces of a Transformer action figure in disguise. "He broke Steeljaw. Listen, Bob," Z said, "I could use a hand rearranging my bookie's feng shui."

"In a minute. Right now I gotta go to the bathroom."

"All right, good luck."

Bobby hurried through the front room into the hall to the bathroom. He did have to piss, but then when he took the large bag of cocaine from under his shirt he forgot all about his raging bladder. He placed the coke on the rusty toilet lid, tore off a corner, his hands trembling as he got in a good snort. His eyes rolled as the drug worked its magic.

"Oh … my … God."

Z barged in on him saying, "Bobby, don't flush the toilet. It's broke."

He saw the bag of cocaine and about went insane.

"Bob! The fuck is that?"

Bobby said, "The fuck does it look like?"

"It looks like a fucking bag of Satan's dandruff is what it is," Z said. "You been holding out on me?"

"It's mine," Bobby said. "I found it in a toilet at the rest stop."

"And you took it?"

"I took it."

Z nodded, giving it some thought before he grinned and said in a milder tone, "You did the right thing."

Bobby, estimating the size of the cocaine, said, "There's about a kilo in here."

"One kilo?" Z said.

It seemed to brighten his eyes, seeing all that cocaine.

"Could be more. I don't know—my math's rusty."

Z dropped to his knees in front of the cocaine as if it were some lost treasure. He said, "It's so beautiful." He looked from the coke to Bobby. "How much does a kilo brick of dope cost?"

Bobby shrugged his bony shoulders. "Oh, about thirty-five to forty years."

Ray and Craig were on Columbus Avenue, and Craig slowed the Hummer to a stop at the light.

Ray said, "Did I tell you I went swimming with dolphins on the weekend? Something I'd never thought I'd do."

"You swam with dolphins?"

"It was a really weird experience. I went to kiss the dolphin, and she slipped her tongue in my mouth."

"On the first date?"

Ray looked at the street they were on and said, "Why are we going this way? We take this route, we'll be late for the strip club."

"All roads lead to one place."

"Yeah, and your asshole isn't one of them."

"We toss," Craig said, went into his pocket, and brought out a quarter. "Heads, we go my way. Tails, we go your way."

Craig tossed the coin. He let it land between the seats and they leaned in to look, bumping heads.

"Ow," Ray said.

"Heads. Ha-ha! I win."

"Damn. I hope to God you don't have lice."

"I guess we're taking the route up my asshole."

The light turned green, and Craig turned off Columbus onto 80th Street and had to give way to pedestrians crossing. When the last of them reached the curb he crawled forward, and they heard a *thud* at the right side of the Hummer.

"Jesus Christ," Craig said. "What idiot walks straight into a Hummer?"

Ray looked out his window at the young man in a hickory golf shirt holding a white cane, which could only mean … Ray said, "A blind idiot," then recognized the young man. "Hey, it's Millicent's brother." Ray was grinning. "I love this kid. He claims he's got two guardian angels. Not one, like everybody else. Two."

"My Hummer!"

Ray said, "It's okay. He didn't dent it."

They heard, "Who's there?"

"Craig."

"Ray."

The young blind guy said, "Make up your mind, is it Ray or Craig?"

"Craig."

"*And* Ray."

"You all right, Shaquille?" Craig said. "Where're you going?"

Shaquille edged to Ray's window. He said, "To my apartment, you know. Nowhere special."

"Hop in," Craig said. "We'll give you a ride."

Shaquille found the rear door, opened it, and struggled to climb into the Hummer. Craig watching.

Saying to him, "Easy does it."

While Craig was distracted, Ray picked up the quarter. "Jumping Jesus on a pogo stick, Craig, this is a two-headed coin. You'd swindle a friend with a two-headed coin?"

"Course," Craig said. "How do you think I got this Hummer?"

A big, round mass of light, an orb, hovered in the air till Shaquille came out of the shower. Shaquille was getting dressed in the bedroom, putting on a fresh T-shirt and jeans before the light made its presence known.

Shaquille opened the doors to his small closet, a hole in the wall. He arranged his golf shirts by their colors: black, gray, blue, green, white, yellow, orange, and red. He picked out an admiral blue golf shirt and black pants and closed the closet. Finally sensing that he wasn't alone in the apartment, Shaquille stopped and cocked his head, listening.

Shaquille waited, he didn't know how long. He didn't hear anything, not a sound, but said it anyway:

"Is somebody here?"

Silence.

No answer. Nothing.

"There's nobody in the apartment. It's all in my blind imagination."

The ghost light floated in the room, moving to and fro.

Shaquille stopped again. "Somebody in here?"

No answer.

Somebody was in the apartment. The hairs standing up on the back of his neck never lied. Shaquille tightened the towel around his waist, crossed the room to the door, and bumped into the wall.

"Hey—who moved the door?"

He felt blindly for the door, located it and stepped out into the hall, trying to detect movement.

"Somebody here?"

No answer.

"If you are, I'd like you to leave. I'm blind. This isn't a fair fight."

Still no answer.

"Please *leave*."

The ghost light drifted out of the doorway behind Shaquille, passing him closely as it made its way into the hall.

"Oh-kay," Shaquille said. "I *felt* that!"

He didn't see the will-o'-the-wisp suspended two feet from him at eye level, beckoning him toward the front door.

Shaquille shook it off and went in the bedroom.

Matthew arrived at the day care center six past four, the place closed, crossed the playroom and stopped at a table.

"Come on out from under the table, Danny."

Matthew stepped back as Danny crawled out from underneath, his pint-sized three-year-old girl. She carried a Kermit the Frog doll, her security object. Kermit's head dangled. It had a rip in the neck that reminded Matthew of Thomas McGinnis.

Danny peered up at her father. She smiled sweetly and said, "Hi, Daddy."

"Another fight? Are you kidding me?"

"I don't start these things."

"And yet you always wind up in them."

She hugged her Kermit doll protectively. "He ripped off Kermit's head."

"Jesus, Danny. You got in a fight wit' a *boy*?"

Danny grew sullen. "He broke Kermit. Bruce is always breaking stuff. You know? That mean, ugly bully."

"You know, the more you talk 'bout this kid, the older he gets."

"Bruce is the paperboy."

Matthew said, "I am very disappointed in you, Danny. Daddy's told you time and time again we don't hit, kick, bite, or push people—not unless they are really asking for it."

Danny said, "I'm sorry, Daddy," in a soft tone, getting the right kind of look to her hazel-brown puppy dog eyes as well.

Matthew didn't give in to that hurt-puppy-dog look; he hung on to his anger. Hung on tight.

"Why are you sorry?"

She shrugged.

"You don't know why you're sorry?"

She raised her head to look at her father again, the hurt-puppy-dog look gone from her eyes. "Tell me why I should be sorry, and I'll be sorry for it later."

There was a tap on the window. Jagger was peeking in through the smudged glass.

Matthew said, "Jesus Christ." He quickly opened the window. "*Jagger?*"

Jagger climbed in. He said, "Hey, Matt," with a grin, and spread his arms out wide at each side. "I finally made it to school."

"How'd you find me?"

"I followed you."

"On foot?"

"No, my ride's outside."

Matthew looked out the window and saw a small, pink scooter. "Where's the little girl that came wit' the scooter?"

"Packed in bubble wrap in the box the scooter came in? How the fuck should I know?"

Matthew put that issue aside. "Jagger, what are you doing out of prison? *Again.*"

"Relax. I'm just out stretching my legs."

Danny said, "Hi, Godfather Jagger."

Jagger smiled at her. "There's my girl, there's my girl." He scooped her up, perched her on the crook of an arm, and pecked her cheek. "How you doing, Princess?"

Danny wrinkled her nose. She said, "You smell. Put me down." Jagger stood her on her head. Danny giggled. "That's my head. Put me on my feet. On my feet."

Jagger set Danny upright. He said, "Man, girls are hard to figure out."

Matthew said, "Tell me 'bout it. She got into a brawl, and she's been suspended for—you ready for this?—two weeks. There goes my quiet alone time."

"Are you surprised Danny's fighting?"

"You saying Danny's acting out because of the divorce?"

"Divorce, demon possession, whatever." Jagger eased into a kiddie chair, looking out of place in his green prison scrubs and telling Matthew to take it easy on Danny. "She's just a baby."

"That's right—she's just a baby. She's got no business fighting. I didn't raise my little girl to fight." Matthew paused, agitated now. "Goddammit, where's her mother?"

Jagger, in the kiddie chair, raised his hand going, "Ooh, ooh, I know where she is."

"You know where she is—" Matthew started to say.

Sirens blared outside and Jagger panicked.

"Uh-oh, shht! Five-o."

He waited until the sirens faded away, then relaxed. "Oh, good, it's not for me."

Matthew looked down at Danny's face turned up to his.

"I gotta say, Matt, she's good."

"Millicent came to me one day as I was training for the championship belt and asked me if I'd teach her to fight," Matthew said. "I was against it. But that little mama knew just how to persuade me."

"Big man like you?"

"Yeah," Matthew said. "I taught her to fight. Now I wish I hadn't. Millicent knows how I feel 'bout her fighting. And don't think I haven't tried to put a stop to it, I have, many times."

"You can't bend the mind of a hard-head."

"The more fights she wins, the deeper she gets drawn in. I should've put my foot down when she had Danny. But I bring it up, and it becomes a problem. The fight would start at the dinner table and end in the bedroom." Jagger grinned. Matthew said, "After that, I never brought it up again. That little woman just don't … give … a … fuck. You know what I'm saying?"

"Yeah," Jagger said. "She's got a tight hold on your dick."

They were among the screaming crowd at a fight club in an abandoned warehouse. They watched two girls as they mercilessly beat each other. One of the girls being Matthew's baby mama, Millicent Dallis-Price, beautiful and petite, feisty, in top shape from excessive training. Millicent spotted them now.

"Uh-oh."

"She sees us."

"She hates me watching," Matthew said. "She says it distracts her game."

As if to prove this theory, a fist slammed into Millicent's face.

"*Ooh*," Jagger said. "She wasn't kidding."

Matthew's cell phone made noise. A butch woman scowled at him over her shoulder and Matthew said, "I don't know whether you're a boy or girl, but nice buzz cut." He found the phone and moved out of the crowd as he answered the call, Jagger following close behind, Matthew saying into the phone, "Talk to me." He listened and said, "In English."

Late November, training for a big fight against Thomas McGinnis to keep his championship belt, Matthew used his customized gymnasium at the manse. He had his cornermen with him and was in the middle of sparring and perfecting his moves when Millicent cut into his training, wanting to have a talk with him. Matthew hunched down and looked at the beautiful young face of his woman through the ropes, smiling at her, showing her a blue rubber gumshield, Millicent saying, "I want you to do something for me." It was the beginning of their relationship, and he was completely infatuated with her, so he was willing to do anything. Matthew listened to Millicent tell him, "I want you to teach me to fight." Except that. Matthew said, "You want me to do *what?*" Maybe he hadn't heard her correctly. "Teach me to fight," Millicent said. "I wanna learn to fight, Matthew."

Matthew remembered thinking, Where did this come from? When he met her, she was working as a cocktail waitress at the Beatrice Inn, Manhattan's hottest nightclub. She'd been seventeen going on eighteen, a beautiful young woman with a heart of gold, a pacifist. And now she wanted to fight. He must've missed something.

Later they were at the manse, cooking dinner. Friday night was the cook's day off, so they cooked together. Sometimes Millicent would wind up on the fourteen thousand-dollar dining table with Matthew eating food off her.

He said, "Why do you want to fight?"

"Do I need a reason?"

"Sure you do," Matthew said. "Nobody fights for no reason."

Millicent said, "Matthew, you're a *boxer*." She was chopping tomatoes with a fucking butcher knife. "I heard a girl got stabbed in her apartment, and I wanna be ready when my turn to die comes."

"Mama, you're not going to die."

"The girl who got stabbed probably thought she wasn't going to die," Millicent said. "Now where is she?"

The thought of him teaching her to box still didn't sit right with him.

Matthew said, "I don't know …"

"You want me to be safe, don't you?"

Matthew took the steak and Irish stout pie from the oven and set it on the marble-topped counter of the kitchen island. He said, "I don't make you feel safe?"

"Matthew, you're not always around, and I get scared."

He knew the kind of trouble fighting could get you into, and he didn't want that for her; he cared about her too much to see her get hurt.

"You don't want to fight, Millicent, believe me."

"I don't *want* to fight," Millicent said, "I wanna *learn* to fight. There's a huge difference." Her voice soft then as she said, "I mean, who better to train me than the undisputed heavyweight champion of the world, huh?" She was working him, saying all the right words to persuade him. Had he allowed himself to surrender to her smooth words, Matthew would be eating out of her hands; or be eating off her, rather.

Matthew had made up his mind. He said, "I'm flattered, but I'm going to have to say no."

That turned off the look. He had disappointed her, and that had cost him Friday night's sex, but he had to make his position clear.

"Fine," Millicent said, though she didn't look fine. "You won't teach me, I'll get someone who will."

And she did. He'd found out who was stupid enough to take her up on her offer. He was at her apartment late one night, waiting for her, with twelve dozen roses and a two weeks old husky puppy. He was there to apologize. Millicent didn't want to hear it and walked past him toward the bedroom. He stopped her, touching her side, and she flinched.

He said, "You alright?"

"Yeah, fine." Her face twisted in pain.

Matthew held onto her side, where the pain was. "What's wrong?"

"Nothing's wrong."

He grew worried, then suspicious. Millicent seemed to be wearing extra layers of clothing. He pulled down the zipper of her lavender hoodie, and spread the sweatshirt opened. There was yet another hoodie. "Two hoodies?" He unzipped the hoodie underneath that saying, "Aren't you hot wit' all these hoodies on?" Man, another one. Matthew rushed to get them all off. Counted one, two, three more hoodies, got to the last one, undid that, and felt immediate panic as he saw the bruise marks on her golden brown skin. "Holy *shit*."

"It only looks bad 'cause I'm new at it, but I will get better."

Matthew said, "Who've you got training you?" His jaw worked. When she didn't respond Matthew said, "Who's fucking training you, Millicent?"

"Thomas McGinnis."

"I won't train you, so you go to the man I am going to fight?"

"I asked, and he was willing."

"Oh, he was willing, was he?" Matthew said, and waited for more.

She didn't say any more.

He felt curious about another matter, and he said, "And while McGinnis is training you, what are you doing for him?"

"I'm letting him train me, aren't I?"

They'd gotten themselves into a bad place over the business of Millicent fighting. He tried to talk her out of it, even to the point of putting his foot down. Millicent, being the stubborn young woman she was, wouldn't listen. She continued to train with McGinnis until Matthew's jealousy and anger erupted in the ring, and it cost a man his life.

He wasn't the only one affected by McGinnis's death, Millicent was taking it harder than him. Matthew didn't understand why it should, McGinnis meant nothing to her. He was gone, and now Millicent had no trainer. That didn't stop her. She trained herself, day and night. She got so hooked that she wouldn't stop. Matthew was watching her on the security monitor: Millicent was hitting that hundred and twenty pounds of heavy bag and getting every throw wrong. Her structure was all messed up. That fucking McGinnis had taught her all wrong. Watching her, Matthew found himself sympathizing with her.

Millicent was going at that bag too aggressively, beating it like it owed her a shitload of money. Then he appeared behind her, close, his body against her sweaty back, and corrected her posture. Matthew saying, "You cannot push, spit, or hit your opponent below the belt." Matthew held Millicent's wrists and raised her hands, the gloves shaped into two fists. "Your hands should be shielding your face at all times. You keep it like that, and you'll walk away wit' all your teeth. McGinnis did that mistake, left his face exposed and took an uppercut to the chin and it snapped his neck." He placed the palm of his hand flat on her tummy and held her closer to him, saying, "If your opponent has a longer reach," moving her in close to the punching bag, "it's essential to move in close. Then you can use a wide range of short hooks and uppercuts to cancel out the reach advantage. You don't want to give him too much access, do you? Close your distance. And always, *always*, protect your face wit' your hands."

She asked him why he was helping her. He told her it was because he loved her and didn't want her to get hurt. He saw the gratitude in those gleaming hazel eyes and was glad, and knew that the relationship was back on an even keel. He leaned in for a kiss, and she raised her hands to her face, fists cocked, blocking access to her full and plumped lips. Millicent saying, "Like this, huh?"

He smiled because, well, she was adorable.

One of the many qualities Matthew loved in his Hawaiian little mama. It turned him on, and he took her right there on the mat. They tore off each other's clothes and made love in the air-conditioned gymnasium.

Though, it didn't take long for her to fall victim. She grew obsessed with fighting. It kicked in around the time she became a young mother. She ignored the baby when it cried for her. Matthew had found his twenty-year-old wife in the gymnasium in the wee hours of the night. He brought the baby to her to be fed, and all Millicent could say was, "Take care of it, okay?" and went back to her training. Matthew said, "The *baby* needs your breasts, Millicent." But no, Millicent didn't have the time.

She was young. It was all about her.

He was with her now in the warehouse restroom, standing at the sink as she cleaned up her cuts, wincing every time she blotted them with disinfectant, Matthew telling his ex-wife about their daughter.

"She fights in day care. She fights because her mommy fights."

Millicent said, "No, she fights 'cause she gets picked on."

"This is serious, Millicent. Our three-year-old daughter could be banned from day care for bad behavior."

"There'll be other day cares."

"Not if this goes on her permanent record. And yes, there is such a thing as a permanent record for a three-year-old. She's just a baby, for Christ's sake."

"A very strong baby," Millicent said, and turned to Matthew, smiling beautifully. "We did good, didn't we?"

Matthew reached out to touch a cut on Millicent's cheekbone, and she right away drew her head from his hand.

"Hey, hey—no, don't get tender with me, Big Boy."

Matthew said, "I hate that I still love you."

Looking into her exotic hazel eyes. Shit.

She said, "Ride home?"

"Where's your car?"

Millicent turned back to the mirror smeared with lipstick. "Had to sell it to pay for the divorce ... fat lot of good that did me."

"That's what you get for picking a lawyer out of the Yellow Pages."

She was staying in a dirt-cheap motel room, practically living there. Matthew took it all in: the dim lighting, the one window, the cramped bathroom, the suitcase on the uncomfortable chair with the broken strapping under the cushion so you fell through, the minibar that was an old cube refrigerator. It tugged at his heart to see the mother of his child living in this dump. He said, "This is where you've been staying?"

"Well, the divorce left me with no money, no place to live, no transportation, no job experience, and some deep emotional scars ..." She looked at him and said, "I'm counting my blessings here, Matthew."

"You could always go to Darryl."

Millicent took a banana from her backpack. "I don't wanna talk about Darryl."

"You don't want to talk 'bout the asshole you had an affair wit'?"

"He was a mistake."

Her hair was up in a ponytail. She pulled out the blue scrunchie and let her hair down. She had a lot of hair, all in jet black curls. And it always smelled nice, like mangoes. He loved mangoes.

"A mistake that's left you divorced and homeless," Matthew said. "He was good enough for you to fuck behind my back, so why not go ask Darryl if he's got a room for you?"

"Well, if it'll make you stop *yell*ing," Millicent said. They got in each other's throat when they were together. She said, "He chose his family over yours truly."

Matthew was composed now. "That did make me stop yelling."

"Bet you're happy seeing me at my lowest."

That hooked him. Matthew scowled.

"Happy? You think this makes me happy? Am I happy the affair is over? Hell yeah. Am I happy seeing you at your lowest?" He paused, said, "Well …" Looked at the mother of his child, now sitting on the side of the double spring bed, and remembered the times he'd come home to find her on her knees on the bed, naked, ready for it. "You didn't think it'd come to this when you opened your legs for him, did you?"

Millicent didn't say anything, peeling her dinner.

"And now he's back wit' his family, and you've lost yours."

She took her time saying, "Are bananas fattening?"

Getting out of discussing her mistake that had ended their marriage.

Matthew saw that the talk of Darryl was over and said, "Well, look at it this way. Have you ever seen a fat monkey?"

She thought about it. "Gorilla."

Z popped a can of Red Bull as he watched a newscast. The good-looking anchorwoman on News 12 giving the latest. "Veteran police officer Jeffrey Hodges, who was working undercover to bring down a drug operation, was found dead in the rest stop on I-87 at four-twenty this afternoon ..."

Z saw the dead cop's photograph, big and bold, on the screen and raised his voice toward the kitchen, "Bob, you gotta come see this."

Bobby's voice came back from the kitchen. "See what?"

"Come and see."

"See what?"

"Fucking get in here!"

Bobby's voice said, "What's going on?" in the living room.

"A narco got shot in the rest stop you found Satan's dandruff."

Bobby shrieked. "A *narco*?"

"Okay, you see, that is why you should stay away from helium balloons."

"Are you kidding me?"

"No, seriously, it's fucked up your voice."

"I'm talking about the narc."

Z said, "Oh," his mind back on the narco. "He was part of an undercover drug bust."

"*Nooo!*"

"*Yesss!*"

Now Bobby looked confused.

"Yes?"

"No!" Z said. "Oh, man, you shouldn't have taken the dandruff. Shoulda left well enough alone."

"You said I did the right thing!"

"To hell with what I said! There's a dead narc in the toilet!"

Bobby gave himself a moment to think before saying, "It's too late to take it back."

"Waaay too late."

Bobby thought some more. "I'll hold on to it."

"May as well."

"Narc's dead."

"He's got no use for it where he's gone. We sell it and split the share."

Was he kidding?

Bobby said, "I ain't gonna just sell one kilogram of Satan's dandruff, Z."

"This could mean life in the slammer."

"No, this could mean making me very happy." Bobby said, "Ooh, wait. My dad's a cop, he'd know what to do."

"Wasn't he killed by a sniper?"

Bobby wilted. "Oh, right …" He said, "There's no way he can help us then."

In the butler's pantry, the French maid was twisting off the bleach cap. It slipped from her fingers and dropped to the floor, where it rolled into the narrow gap between the two cabinets. She couldn't reach it. She settled for a drinking glass on the shelf and picked out a Kermit the Frog jelly glass.

The kitchen phone rang.

The butler called to her from in there, "Roselle, answer the phone."

Rushing from the pantry, the maid put the jelly glass on the counter and picked up the wall phone. She said, "Piars residence."

Danny ran in. "Hi, Nood."

The butler smiled pleasantly at her. "Hello, Miss Danielle."

"Can I please have some water?"

"Absolutely."

The butler walked to the refrigerator and Danny, seeing her jelly glass on the counter with liquid in it, took it saying, "Never mind."

She innocently drank the bleach.

The butler came back with a glass of water and watched her put the jelly glass down, empty now. Danny wiped her mouth with the back of her hand.

He looked alarmed. "Miss Danielle, did you just *drink* the bleach?"

"That water tasted yucky." Danny paused and said, "My throat hurts."

Matthew was on the bedroom terrace, asking the stars for advice. "I wanted to believe I was doing right by taking full custody of my daughter. She's better off wit' me. Am I wrong? I'm her father." Matthew said, "I'm her sole provider, and her mother's barely working. She's not fit for it." He paused to gaze at the starred sky. "Am I doing the right thing?" He sighed. "I could really use a sign right now."

Nothing happened.

"Totally up to you." Staring at the stars.

Then the doorbell chimed: his sign, as requested.

Matthew stared at the heavens. He said, "You're not bad," uncertain now. "And now I'm little scared."

He opened the etched glass front door to Jagger and Millicent on the high cobblestone porch.

116

Matthew said to Millicent, "Didn't I leave you at the motel?"

"I came to get my things."

Jagger said, "And I came to get whatever she breaks."

Z was on the phone to his bookie.

"Look, Chic-Keane, I ain't trying to put off paying you. You'll have your money by tonight. Would I lie to you?" Z said, "Okay, I would. But right now I'm telling the truth." Z said, "Okay, I'm not." He said, serious now, "I'll have your money … No, really."

He hung up and searched for the cocaine—under the couch, behind the TV, in the kitchen cabinets. He didn't find it anywhere.

"Dammit. Where'd he put it?"

Z came to the bathroom, Bobby was in there showering. Z rapped on the door.

"Yo, Bob? Where'd you put the coke?"

Bobby popped his head out the door. "I put the last can in the fridge."

It got Z frustrated. "The *cocaine*. Where is it? Chic-Keane will show up in a couple hours. Give me a pinch I can sell to make me some dough."

Bobby hesitated. "I returned it to the cops."

Z squinted at him saying, "You returned the dandruff?" Surprised and then shaking his head, refusing to accept it. "No, no, no. You didn't."

"Damn," Bobby said. "I was so sure you'd believe that lie."

He shouldn't have hesitated.

"It's somewhere in the apartment," Z said, "and you gonna bring it to me. Don't make me go through you to get it."

Bobby retrieved the cocaine from the toilet tank. There was rat poison behind the bowl. He snatched it up and hid it in his pants pocket.

Z was anxiously pacing back and forth as Bobby returned with the dope.

"Aight, Z, here's the dandruff, all of it."

Z took the cocaine. As he turned away to admire it, Bobby spilled a few drops of rat poison into Z's Red Bull and then slipped the poison back in his pants, Z talking to himself.

"I'm gonna sell this and pay off my brother once and for all—" He reconsidered. "Naw, I'll write him an IOU."

Bobby stood back. "Remember, Z, half of that dandruff's mine."

Z came around then.

"Huh?"

Looking at Bobby, forgot all about him.

Z said, "Oh, Bob."

"You sell the coke, you're gonna split the share."

"Split the share?"

Z reached around behind him and brought out a Browning .45 from the waist of his pants hanging on his ass.

Z said, "I gotta say—that doesn't sound like something I would *nor*mally do."

Bobby put his palms out saying, "Hey, now—"

And *bam*, Z popped him.

Z put the Browning away, his eyes rolling with insanity. "No, this is all mine."

Admiring his stash, he drank his laced Red Bull.

Millicent breezed into the kitchen, Matthew and Jagger in tow. Jagger asked the butler, "What's for dinner, Nood?"

The maid blurted out, "Danielle drank bleach!"

It stopped her parents. Both of them said, "*What?*" Their voices sharp with alarm.

Jagger said, "I'm not in the mood for bleach. You got any leftover lasagna?"

"Oh my God!" Millicent ran to her child.

Matthew yelled at the maid. "Weren't you watching her?"

"I answered a call."

"Call poison control! *Now*, Roselle!"

"*Oui, Monsieur.*"

The French maid raced to the phone and punched a number.

"No time," Millicent said. "Give me the African red oil, Nood."

119

The butler got a big bottle of red palm oil from the cabinet and brought it to her.

"Danny, drink this," Millicent said. "The red oil will counteract the poison."

Matthew said, "Try olive oil."

"Olive oil is for *before* being poisoned. Red palm oil is for *after*—you know, when it's all too late."

Jagger said, "She's right."

"'Course I am."

Jagger looked off then, into space. He said, "Put some pressure on the wound."

Matthew looked over.

"Say what?"

"I was talking to Bobby," Jagger said, and walked out.

Millicent was saying to Danny, "Okay, sweetie, how do you feel now?"

"My throat's not hurting," Danny said, and belched loudly.

Z was sprawled in the doorway, as if he had attempted to leave the apartment, but never quite made it out the door before the poison took him. Bobby bled out on the living room floor, barely conscious. Jagger, in the room, knelt beside him.

"Bobby? Bobby?" Jagger saw the life draining out of Bobby's eyes. "No, no, no. Stay with me, all right?"

Bobby was going.

"Bob!"

With a blood-stained hand, Jagger punched a number into the telephone, his thumb slipping on the dial. "Hang in there, kid."

Shaquille was sitting on the couch while having dinner.

He said to himself, "I could be eating monkey brains, and I wouldn't know."

The ghost light appeared in the living room, and the hairs on the back of Shaquille's neck stood up.

"I'm getting that feeling …"

He detected movement close to him.

The ghost light made no sound. It hovered and glowed as it moved toward Shaquille.

Shaquille's head turned, and the ghost light receded.

"Who's there?"

No answer. He resumed his meal.

Shaquille felt heat circle him and then move away. The ghost light stopped at the front door to the apartment.

"Why won't you leave me alone with my food?" He wrapped his fingers around the hilt of a knife, ready to strike the intruder. "I don't know what you want from me." He gave a wild yell—"*Hiyah!*"—the kind of sound you made doing karate. He swept the knife at the air in front of him.

The ghost light floated beyond his reach.

Not even close.

Shaquille saying, "Come on, fight me! Fight me!"

Nothing.

"Coward." Shaquille turned his head toward the ghost light, not more than two feet away. "I know where you are. I feel you." He paused, said, "Where are you?" Not so sure exactly.

He felt a strong energy that was warm and harmless. His fear diminished.

"You're not human." Realizing it now.

He extended a hand toward the light. The will-o'-the-wisp receded.

"*What* are you?"

No answer.

Shaquille's hand remained extended toward its energy. He said, "I can feel you."

The ghost light moved away, making a beckoning gesture.

"What is it? I'm blind. What do you want with me?"

The energy of the ghost light tugged Shaquille forward, like elastic, and he willed himself to track it.

He was beginning to understand. "You want me to follow you."

As if on an invisible leash, the ghost light pulled the blind man along.

"I'm coming. I'm—" He coughed.

The ghost light guided Shaquille out of the apartment building. Cold night air hit him. Shaquille frowned, confused. He said, "You brought me outside."

The ghost light departed, rising ever higher into a domed sky full of winking stars.

A woman ran out of her house in her slippers, calling out to him, "Shaq!"

Shaquille turned toward the sound of her voice.

"Pamela?"

Pamela cinched her robe around her and hunched her shoulders in the cold. "Oh my *God*. Shaquille, are you okay?"

"Course I'm okay. Why wouldn't I be?"

"Because," Pamela said, "your apartment is on fire!"

SOMEBODY WALKED OVER MY GRAVE

Shaquille was strapped to a gurney in the back of an ambulance. Pamela sat close by while two paramedics worked on him. He'd fainted from the shock of almost being burned down with his apartment.

The female paramedic brought out a scalpel and Pamela was on her. "Is that scalpel really necessary?"

The female paramedic scratched nail polish off her fingernail with the scalpel. "It gets the nail polish off."

Shaquille jolted awake. "Save me from this cruel world!"

"He's awake," Pamela said. "Shaq, are you okay?"

"Depends. What am I lying on?"

"A gurney."

"Oh, so I'm not lying in hell on a grill over a fire, and the devil isn't prodding me with his pitchfork?"

Pamela said, "No. You're in an ambulance, among mankind."

Shaquille stiffened with panic. "Ambulance? We haven't left the apartment?"

"It's still outside, burning to the ground."

"Good, there's still hope. Get me off this thing."

"Shaq, are you sure?"

"Get me off the gurney. Where are the straps?"

Pamela guided his hand to them. "They're right here."

He began undoing the strap. Pamela worked on the other one. That didn't set well with the paramedics.

The female paramedic asked what was wrong with him, couldn't he see? Pamela told her he was blind. The male paramedic wanted to know, "From the fire?" Shaquille told him from birth, and said, "Now get me off this gurney!"

The straps were undone. Pamela took hold of Shaquille by his upper arm. She said, "There you go," nice and easy, helping him off the gurney so he wouldn't walk in his own puke—step around it, good—out of the ambulance. No, the paramedics wouldn't have that.

The male paramedic saying, "Sir, I'd advise you let us take you to the hospital."

"Providing you called me sir, I'm gonna tell you nicely," Shaquille said—yelling at him—"*Back off.*" Pleasantly then. "Okay?"

"Please, sir?"

"Don't push your luck!"

Shaquille's hand touched the paddles. That gave him pause.

"Paddles. Man, these are cool. Are they on?"

The male paramedic nudged his partner in the arm with his elbow, sneaking a look between them.

"Why don't you try it?"

He switched on the paddles.

The building's other tenants were out in the street, watching firefighters attempt to put out the fire in Shaquille's apartment. Shaquille and Pamela were out of the ambulance now.

"That sneak switched the paddles on, didn't he?"

Pamela said yeah, and asked Shaquille why he didn't let them take him to the hospital.

"While I was out, I dreamed the ambulance crashed." He didn't consider whether he should tell her.

Pamela said, "You're kidding." She paused and said, "Blind people dream?"

The O strip club was full tonight, strippers grinding poles, the VIP rooms active with celebrities and high rollers. Ahmed sauntered to the bar that was tended by gorgeous lady bartenders. He blended into the crowd of multicolored people with his dark hair and dark Mediterranean skin. A bowl of mixed nuts sat on the counter. Ahmed scooped a handful and popped them in his mouth as he stared at the good-looking strippers, thongs digging into their butt cracks. A guy in a gold aviator sunglasses started to reach for the nuts, and Ahmed locked his hand around the guy's wrist.

"Whoa, man! Your hand kinda got away from you there."

The guy in the aviator sunglasses looked as though he was having a hard time sticking to an expression. He said, "Uh, no, it didn't."

Ahmed said, "Uh, yes, I believe it did."

"I just want some nuts, dude."

"Oh, you want nuts, so you grab mine, uh?"

That went by him.

"Excuse me?"

Ahmed said, "Don't you have your own nuts?"

"Hey, listen. I'm sorry. I thought they were for everybody."

"Nooo, man, not my nuts."

"What is your problem, dude?"

"My problem," Ahmed said, "is that a guy with his own nuts has no business grabbing another man's nuts."

The break room had the essentials: free coffee, lunch tables with delicious snacks and your choice of healthy food options, games, comfortable furniture, television, and the occasional staff celebration. In actuality, the bouncers spent more time in here.

Giber was looking through *Men's Fitness* on the couch, turning pages, his titanium cobalt ring gleaming on his thumb. He said, "You know what this magazine is missing? Big-ass bitches."

Monk walked in, late as usual.

Lyndon said, "Jesus Christ, Monk, you're two hours late."

"Ah see, I'm getting better," Monk said. "Yesterday I was three hours late."

Andrew, at the counter pouring coffee, said, "You keep showing up late for work."

"I try coming early, but that never quite works out."

"Well, give it time," Giber said, his nose in the magazine. "You'll get used to going out after sundown."

Monk took off his tweed cap. "Is the boss in?"

"The boss is *always* in." Lyndon, buzz cut hair in a swirling razor pattern, turned to his fellow bouncer Urban beside him, and said, "You cutting the right brake line?"

"Yeeeah," Urban said.

The walkie-talkie on the low table in front of the couch made a static noise. They listened to Virgil's sonorous, black Southern voice say, "Calling for backup!"

Urban said, "I think Darth Vader's trying to channel through."

Lyndon picked up the walkie-talkie and pressed his thumb on the button to speak into it. He said, "What's up, Virgil?"

"I got two douche dicks fighting at the bar. From what I was able to piece together, one of 'em tried to grab the other one's nuts."

Andrew grumbled. "God, I can't put my feet up for one minute."

Lyndon said into the walkie, "Andrew's on his way."

Virgil came back with, "Oh, well then, I suggest the rest of you ninnies pull your heads out of each other's asses and follow Andrew!"

Ahmed and the guy in the aviator sunglasses were wrestling on the floor. Virgil and another bouncer tried to peel them off each other as the rest of the bouncers rushed in and gave a hand.

"All right, ladies," Virgil said. They pulled them apart. "Now, what's going on, huh?"

Ahmed said, "This guy tried to grab my nuts."

Virgil looked at the other guy, the guy's aviator sunglasses askew.

Virgil said to him, "Is that true, sir? Did you try to grab this man's nuts?"

"I just wanted something to nibble on."

Ahmed said, "Try a pacifier."

The guy in the sunglasses lunged at Ahmed, and Virgil pulled him back.

"That's it, you're out of here," Virgil said, and dragged the dude with his aviator sunglasses along the bar to the club room entrance.

Ahmed said, "Asshole'll never try to grab my nuts again."

The four bouncers sat around talking. Lyndon said, "The stinky seaman from Lake Erie."

Giber said, "Oh yeah, I didn't smell that coming. Never pick a fight with a seaman. He just might slap you with a fish."

Ahmed said, sitting with them, "That must've hurt the fish."

He had their attention, the bouncers looking right at him.

Andrew said, "Hey, look. It's the guy who got his nuts grabbed by that other guy."

"Okay, you got your free coffee," Lyndon said to Ahmed. "You freaked everybody out. Now leave."

"I can't leave."

"Why not?" Urban said. "Is the chair stuck to your ass?"

"I work here."

"You don't work here." Urban said to his fellow bouncers, "He's yanking our chain."

Lyndon looked at Ahmed. "Of all the things you could've yanked, you had to go yank my chain."

"If you're a bouncer," Andrew said to Ahmed, "why aren't you in your uniform?"

"It's at the dry cleaners."

"Which dry cleaners?"

"The one with all the washing machines in it."

The bouncers looked at each other.

"Come on—it's me, Ahmed. With a silent *h*."

Giber asked his fellow bouncers, "Do any you guys know any Ahmeds with a silent *h*?"

"No," Urban said. "But I know a psychic with a silent *p*."

"You seriously don't remember me?"

No, it didn't look like it.

Ahmed said, "Man, you take three days off work and everybody forgets you."

Lyndon said to him, "You work here at the O, prove it. Where's your locker?"

Lyndon and Andrew were with Ahmed in the locker room, staring at the rows of one tier lockers.

"Now before I show you my locker," Ahmed said, "I'd just want to ask, where *is* my locker?"

"You don't know where your locker is?" Lyndon said.

"Course I know where my locker is. It's my locker." Ahmed pointed to a locker at random. "It's right there."

Andrew said, "That's my locker."

"Does it have your name on it?"

"Yes." Andrew pointed to the tag. "There it is. An- . . . *drew*."

"If you don't have a locker," Lyndon said to Ahmed, "you must not work at the O."

"I don't understand. I left my locker right here."

"Sorta like I left my heart in San Francisco," Andrew said.

"I'm telling you," Ahmed said, "I work here. I have for two centuries."

Andrew frowned. "You mean two years."

"Close enough."

Andrew looked at Lyndon now.

"What do we do?"

"Dunno," Lyndon said. "We're gonna have to take this to the boss."

"Boss ain't gonna like this."

Lyndon said, "No, he's not." He paused, said, "Lemme know how he takes it," and escaped from the room.

Soon as he had brought the ambulance to a halt at the curb, the male paramedic got out, retrieved his medical bag from the back, and ran through the open gates. He found the victim, an older man, slumped against a stone, bleeding from a stab wound in the abdomen. The knife was still in him. An emotional younger man faced him. There were a few feet of overgrown grass between them.

The younger man was saying, "You know this is the last place I thought you'd wind up."

The male paramedic pushed past him, saying, "Excuse me." He said to the older man, "We'll take care of you, sir."

He didn't waste time beginning treatment.

"What happened here?"

"If you don't know by looking at me," the older man said, "you're in the wrong business."

"What's your name, sir?"

"Paul St. George."

The male paramedic raised his eyebrows with a small smile.

"Paul St. George? That's an unusual name."

"What's your name, dingleberry?"

"Leslie Case."

"And what was it before someone changed it?"

The male paramedic told himself to be nice and said, "All right, Mr. St. George, I'm going to need for you to breathe calmly."

"Breathing is all I've been doing before you got here."

"Sir, I don't want you to panic. Everything looks good."

"The fact that I have a knife sticking out of my gut makes me look good? Some Leslie Case you are."

"You don't seem to have lost too much blood. It's fortunate you left the knife in. It may be what's keeping you alive."

He smiled to get the older man to relax.

"You're gonna be okay."

"All right, but the second I see you pull out the catheter, it's my foot up your ass."

Threatening him, with a knife in him.

Leslie checked the older man's temperature.

Leslie said, after, "Christ, your skin is cold."

"Well, I *have* been lying here for sixteen weeks."

It threw him off.

"What?"

The older man said, "Half an *hour*." He said, "You don't hear so good?"

Leslie got a stethoscope from his medical bag, stuck the earpieces into his ears, and placed the disk-shaped resonator against the older man's hairy chest. The older man shivered.

"Don't you people ever think to heat that thing?"

Leslie's brow creased in concentration.

The older man stirred against the stone as the paramedic said, "I can't seem to find a heart beat."

"All right, this is getting all too real for my taste."

"How are you still alive when you have no heartbeat?"

The older man kept quiet. Let him figure it out.

Leslie remembered the younger man and looked around at him—a white male in dark clothes, mid to late twenties, measuring at five-ten, and about a hundred and eighty pounds. The guy hadn't moved. He looked in their direction, holding his tongue.

"Sir?"

Didn't get a reply.

Leslie looked at the older man. "Is he deaf? Deaf and mute?"

"He's not deaf. Or mute."

"Then why doesn't he answer?"

The older man said, "Because he can't hear you," and said, "He's still not deaf."

"What's going on?"

Leslie raised a hand to nudge the younger man, get his attention, and his hand passed into him.

"What the hell?"

Then he noticed the stone. It was a tombstone with a name and date inscribed on it.

Paul St. George

1934–2015

Loving father and grandfather

Leslie's eyes and Paul St. George's eyes locked.

Paul St. George growled. "Get off my grave."

The younger man spoke to the older man's tombstone. "The whole family still grieves for you, Granddad."

Leslie gave his surroundings a scan and realized now he was in a cemetery and his partner wasn't with him.

He said, "Jenny?"

Frightened, he packed up his equipment and left the older man lying there.

The younger man stared at the tombstone. The ground on the grave was empty. "Rest easy, Granddad."

The room was called the Eye in the Sky, the strip club's version of an observation room. It resembled a crawl space except here you could stand upright. From the catwalk you could look twenty feet down to the club room directly below. Craig stood in the middle of the wide catwalk, leaning against the handrail and drinking on the job. Andrew climbed the metal stairway and came up to him.

"Hey, boss. When'd you get here?"

"Andrew, I got here an hour ago," Craig said. "You held the door open for me? You asked me how my weekend went?"

Andrew nodded, remembering. "Right, right. Your weekend of body painting with your wife." He watched Craig swigging a beer and said, "You're not supposed to drink on the job, boss."

"What did you call me?"

"Boss."

"That's right, I'm the boss," Craig said. "And the definition of boss is what?"

"Asshole?"

"It's 'Do whatever you want.'"

"And what's the definition of employee?"

"'Do whatever your boss says.'"

"So the boss gets his own way."

"And it brings us back."

"Listen, boss?" Andrew paused, Craig's attention was somewhere else. "What are you doing?"

"Watching people down below going about their lives as if the world isn't going to end tomorrow. This must be what God does when He needs a good laugh."

This didn't concern Andrew, the cultured and humble bouncer. He said, "Boss, we got a guy who claims he works at the club, but nobody recognizes him."

"What's his name?"

"Ahmed. Ahmed Adoodie."

It took all of a moment for Andrew to explain the weird look Craig was giving him. It was the name Ahmed Adoodie. Like saying, *I made a doodie.*

Andrew said, "And I've just realized why I'm standing here and Lyndon isn't."

They ganged up on Ahmed, who was sitting on the bench in the locker room. Craig said to him, "All right, Ahmed, what is your real name?"

"My real name is Kenny Dewitt."

Like saying, *Can he do it?*

Craig said, "Are you messing with me?"

"No, I'm saying Kenny Dewitt."

Craig didn't care for what this guy was doing, making them look stupid.

Lyndon said, "You want me to throw him out?"

"You can't throw me out. I work here."

Andrew sounded tired saying to Craig, "He says that a lot."

"That's because I work here."

"See what I mean?"

Craig saw he'd better put an end to this.

"I'm the head bouncer at this strip club," Craig said. "I've memorized every face of my bouncers and Kenny Dewitt is not one of them. You don't belong here."

The guy with the two names turned his head, raising his hands in a kind of helpless gesture.

"It's high school all over again."

Craig waited.

Why?

Lyndon spoke up. "Boss?"

"Toss him out in the trash with Mel Gibson," Craig said.

"You do that, and I'll sue this strip club."

Craig said, "Oh, well, that takes the fun out of it." Did he seriously think that would work?

Andrew and Lyndon rushed the guy on the bench with the two names, two of them taking him by surprise, grabbing the guy by his arms between them, lifting him off the bench and rushing him away, his shoes dragging along the floor. The guy was resisting.

"All right, all right, my real name is Otis Berne."

It caught Andrew and Lyndon before they could throw him out.

The guy pulled away.

They let him.

The guy said, "You're Craig McCane. You're from Dublin, you were born on April Fools', and you like taking long walks on the beach." He added in a tedious tone, "Long, *long* walks." Serious again. "Your wife's Joanna. She's eight months pregnant with your son, and she hates it when you cluck like a chicken before bedtime."

Lyndon was at a loss. "Who are you talking about?"

Craig said, "*Me*," an edge to his tone. "He's talking about *me*."

The guy expected to get something out of this … whatever *this* was. Even getting personal by bringing in Craig's wife and unborn son.

Lyndon said to Craig aside, Otis watching them from the bench, "Long walks on the beach?"

"It's a guilty pleasure, all right?" Craig said. "I get a lot of stress from working, you guys aren't exactly easy to take, and walking on the beach relieves that stress. And plus, I like how the sand feels between my toes and the way the moonlight shines on the ocean."

"Does the moonlight make you want to dance?"

"Shut up. It's a beautiful thing. Something I quite enjoy, and I don't see how the *fuck* this asshole could've known."

Andrew said, "When I wanna know about a woman, I go through her underwear draw." They looked at him, and he said, "I didn't say that."

Craig shook his head, he had no time for this shit. "I'm just gonna ask him calmly and politely to *piss off.*"

They came around and found themselves staring into the deadly muzzle of a .45 Colt revolver pointed at them.

Otis had them where he wanted.

Craig said, "Is he pointing a Colt at us?"

Andrew and Lyndon answered yes, indeed he was.

Craig said, "All right," shrugging, like what can you do. He asked Otis, "What do you want?"

"First of all," Otis said, "I wanna know who's the boss."

Lyndon right away jerked his head to Craig. "He's the boss."

The Colt moved a couple of inches to aim directly at Craig. Otis said, "Are you the boss?"

Craig nodded. Might as well admit it.

"I'm the boss."

Otis thumbed back the hammer, and again leveled it on Craig.

"Are you really the boss?"

There was a way out of this. Craig said, "You must be talking about *my* boss."

Monk barged in. He gasped when he saw the Colt.

"I'm sorry, I meant to pick door number two," Monk said, and backed out the door, shutting it.

Craig asked Monk in the hall, "Did you make the call?" in an urgent tone. Monk said he sure did, and Craig said, "What did they say?"

"They said the pizza will be here in fifteen minutes."

"Pizza?"

Monk said, "Yeah, I ordered the limburger." A big stupid grin on his open and guileless face.

Wait.

Craig said, "You didn't call the cops?"

Obviously not. "Nooo."

"Why not?"

"It looked like you had it all under control," Monk said. "I didn't want to provoke the situation."

"Monk, the guy in there has got a Colt!"

Monk said, "Yeah, I saw that," sounding surprised now to realize it.

"He's holding Andrew and Lyndon hostage till I get my boss, and you're telling me you didn't call the cops?"

Monk heard the urgency rise in his boss's voice and didn't know how to handle it.

"Well, gee—boss, you want me to call the cops?"

Monk sounding like he didn't want to move his mouth.

"That would be fucking swell, yes!"

He found Ray behind the U shaped office desk, shaking an empty Pringles can over his upturned mouth.

Craig made a *cuckoo* sound in his throat.

And Ray startled. He saw Craig at the door and said, "Oh hey, it's you. I thought you were the cuckoo bird from my clock, but I smashed that to pieces with a hammer."

"Listen, Ray, we have a problem. There's this really uptight guy in the locker room that wants to speak with the boss and, oh, yeah, he's sporting a loaded Colt .45."

Ray said, "Is he an employee?"

Craig said, "I'm almost definitely sure he isn't."

"He's got a loaded Colt .45 and he's not an employee?"

"No."

"He's got a loaded Colt .45 and he wants to talk to me?"

"Yeah."

"Why me?"

The man losing his cool.

"Well, because—thankfully—you are the boss."

"What should I do?"

"You're the boss," Craig said, "so go and talk to the crazy gunman. Let him do what he wants to you. Get this over with."

Andrew and Lyndon stood against the lockers with Otis pointing the Colt at them. Lyndon's nose twitched. He said, "Can I ask permission to scratch my nose?"

"No," Otis said.

Lyndon said, "Cool." He pushed his bottom lip forward and blew air up at his nose to sooth the itch. It didn't help.

"Stop that."

Lyndon became still.

Craig led Ray into the locker room, Craig saying to Otis, "Okay, I brought my boss. He's the one you really want."

Otis looked at Ray. "Are you the boss?"

Ray said yes he was. "Are you the uptight man with the Colt .45?"

Otis leveled the Colt in their direction. Both bosses stiffened.

Craig said to Ray, "Don't make fun of him."

"Right," Ray said, and asked Otis, "So, what did you want to talk to me about?"

Otis said, "I want a job."

Ray looked surprised. They all did.

Ray saying, "You want a job?"

"Wait one cotton-picking minute," Craig said. "That's what you want? A job?"

Otis said, "Yes."

Ray said, "Listen, man, if a job was what you wanted, why didn't you ask instead of getting your little friend to do it?"

"I did. But see, when an ex-con comes back to town, suddenly there's no open position anywhere on the East Coast."

"And you really think the best way to get a job is to hold the employers at gunpoint?"

"I took the alternative approach and that got me two middle fingers, a bucket of acid, and a face full of phlegm."

Craig said, trying to show his interest now, "You had a bucket of acid thrown on you just for asking for a job?"

Lyndon said, "Yeah, man, didn't you think to *duck* out of the way?"

"Being nice gets you nowhere in this world," Otis said, his voice rising in anger and frustration. "But lucky for me—I know how to play the game." He told them straight, "I want a job and I'm not leaving here without one."

Did he seriously think it was that simple?

Ray said, "Oh, but I can't hire you. It's not in my power."

Otis put the Colt back on Craig. He said, "You said he was the boss."

"I am the boss," Ray said. "But I, too, have a boss."

Otis said, "Are you shitting me?"

"We all answer to a higher power."

"You're telling me now I gotta go through *your* boss if I want to work?"

"'Fraid so, man."

Otis exploded in anger. "*Well, go get him! Go get him!*"

Ray kept his cool, telling the crazy guy with the loaded Colt revolver, "You could try asking me nicely."

Otis cocked the Colt, for effect, for the sound of it, and Ray lost his cool for the second time tonight.

"Nicely said."

Ray walked out of the locker room.

Craig said, "I'll go with you," starting to follow him.

Otis yelled at him, "Stay where you are!"

Craig's shoes skidded as he stopped, puzzled, frowning at Otis.

"I want you as collateral," Otis said. He motioned with the Colt, a flick of the wrist, for Craig to get in line with Andrew and Lyndon against the lockers.

It was late now. The gate was open as Leslie ran to it. No, it was closed, he believed, from the wind blowing it shut. He pushed against it and discovered that it wasn't only closed; it was locked.

The older man, an apparition, appeared beside him.

"The gates are locked."

Leslie jumped at the voice. "Well, open it."

"I don't have the key."

Leslie looked out into the street. The ambulance he'd driven here was gone.

"Where's the ambulance?"

"There was never an ambulance," the older man said. "And the gate was never open. If it had been, do you think we'd still be here?"

"Make sense, old man."

"You're dead."

Leslie didn't speak for a moment, staring at him.

"I'm not dead."

"Have you forgotten the accident? The one that brought you here?" The older man paused but didn't get a reaction. "Come on, dingleberry, use your memory box."

He watched the paramedic shake his head.

"I wasn't in an accident—" Leslie cut himself off, starting to remember. "Oh, something's coming to me."

The older man prompted him. He said, "An apartment burned down."

"We had triple casualties. We were taking a blind guy to the hospital, but he didn't want to go. We got a report at 8:30—a second casualty in front of a strip club, an accident victim, hostage suspect, some loser. Got run over by a squad car. He didn't make it. We lost him at 9:05. Another call came in while we were on the road, a mugging victim at Greenwood." Leslie paused as events became clear. "The accident happened on our way to Greenwood."

He had driven the ambulance while his partner worked on the strip club victim in back. Headed toward them was an Alhambra, moving in the same direction as the ambulance. The Alhambra's driver crashed into the ambulance. The ambulance careened off the road and into a bakery truck parked in front of the Fifth Avenue Market, killing him. "I remember Jenny calling out to me." Calling to him from within the wreckage. "I could hear her. She was screaming my name. The girl had great set of lungs on her," he told the older man. "And I wanted to answer her, only I couldn't."

The older man said, "Because you were gone."

"I died in the accident." He paused, the reality hitting him. Then frowning, a look of resentment, saying, "I died, and she lived."

"I know," the older man said, sharing his resentment. "Why does fate always pick the chick to live?"

Matthew said, "Who is he?"

"Otis Berne."

"I don't know him."

"Nobody on Planet Compos Mentis knows this wacko."

"And he wants a job?"

Ray said, "Baaad."

They were in the club's surveillance room watching Otis on camera. Ray, wearing shirtsleeves with a necktie, his suitcoat on the back of the desk chair in the office, watched Matthew inspect the locker room monitor. The big guy was in his winter coat, over a T-shirt and sweatpants, Matthew having been called down here at the last minute.

The cocktail waitress, Paige, a knock-out, tanned, brought Matthew his drink. Scotch neat, his usual.

"For you, Big Boss," Paige said.

Matthew took the drink from the tray and smiled. "Paige, you spoil me."

"Yeah? Well, you get me all moist." So smitten you could smell her lust.

She left them.

Watching her go Ray felt a stir in his pants. He glanced down and said to his crotch, "Down, boy. I know you like her"—looking up—"I like her too."

Matthew stared at the monitors. "Danny drank a cup of bleach earlier."

"Jesus Christ, is she okay?"

Matthew's gaze moved from the monitors to Ray. "She's fine. Millicent tried a home remedy involving African red palm oil. And it worked. The paramedic said Danny'll live. Till the next incident. And then the dog thanked him by peeing on his leg."

"Thank God she's all right."

"Yeah." Matthew paused and said, "African red oil," with a tone of incredulity. "I should've known that—and I'm from Africa."

Ray, the Jamaican American, said, "I feel *I* should've known."

Matthew brought his mind back to Otis. "Doesn't the numbnuts know that's not the way to ask for what you want?"

"He's learning as he goes along."

"Something he and my mom had in common." Matthew straightened. "Alright."

"What do you plan to do?"

"I plan on having sex wit' a hooker tonight."

That wasn't what he meant. Ray said, "What do you plan to do with *Otis*?"

Matthew said, "I'm not really into threesomes."

"The *hostage* situation, Matt."

"Oh. I won't know till I get in there."

"By then it'll be too late."

Ray's eyes went to the monitor showing Otis, and moved close to get a better look, his gaze holding onto the Colt. There was something about the revolver that didn't look right.

"Matt, you're the gun enthusiast. Does that Colt .45 look normal to you?"

Matthew looked with him. "Well, no, but that's only 'cause it's a …"

"It's a what?"

Ray saw Matthew give him that look. I should've known. Like he couldn't believe they had been swindled by this fool.

Matthew walked out without saying anything.

Monk stood next to the locker room door, guarding the way in, as Ray and Matthew walked up to him.

Monk said, "Hey, Big Boss."

Matthew didn't answer him, something coming to mind. "Where are the cops in all of this?"

"I called them," Monk said. "Just want to clarify that."

"That was forty-five minutes ago." Ray looked at his watch. "And it's now—"

Coming up the long narrow hall, Urban heard Monk say, "Midnight." Urban said, "Midnight? I promised my godmother I'd be back home before midnight." And rushed back the other way.

Monk raised his hand to show Matthew and Ray his watch, turning it in the light. "Like my new watch? Went out and bought it an hour ago."

Matthew turned on him. "You left in the middle of work to go and buy a watch?"

"I saw my chance, and I took it. What would you do?"

"Monk," Matthew said coolly, "I'm paying to keep your mother on life support. Do you seriously want to know what the fuck I would do?"

He pushed through the door to the locker room.

Ray came in behind him.

Soon as they walked in the door Otis put the Colt on Matthew. Otis saw the guy was built like a fucking dump truck. Matthew took his time checking out Otis. Otis held the Colt on him. After all, he was the Big Boss. Now the Big Boss stared, not doing anything. Otis believed the man was thinking how he could take the Colt from him without getting his brains blown out. The man could sure as hell stare. He looked Otis right in the face with his piercing blue eyes. Otis stared back. He made sure not to blink. You wouldn't want to take your eye off this guy for a second. The man moved. Otis watched the Big Boss slowly slip a hand into his jacket. Otis raised the Colt, ready to shoot if the Big Boss made the wrong move. The Big Boss didn't look stupid, but tough situations made even the smartest people react stupidly sometimes.

Matthew took his cell phone out. He punched a number. The Colt remained firmly on him even as he raised the phone to his ear. But then when Matthew said, "We found him," Otis bolted for the door and dropped the Colt, almost tripping on his way out.

The tension now relieved, Ray picked up the Colt. He said, "This is a fake gun. I asked you about the Colt and you knew right away it was fake, huh?"

Lyndon looked out the door and then said to Matthew, "Oh, shit, you made him piss himself."

"Who did you call?" Craig said.

Matthew put the call on and a voice said out of the speaker.

"Hello? Domino's Pizza … Hello?"

Andrew and Lyndon came out the locker room together, Lyndon telling Andrew, "Watch out for the piss puddles."

The three bosses were next out the door.

"I can't believe I never thought of that," Ray said. "Show no fear."

They heard "Psst."

Jagger was down the hall, lurking in the shadows. He watched them come toward him.

Craig smiled, pleased to see him.

"Hey, Jagger."

Matthew said, "Good news. Danny's going to be okay."

Ray saw a red stain on the front of Jagger's prison attire. "I see you put ketchup on everything too."

"It's not ketchup," Jagger said. "It's blood."

Matthew said, "Whose blood is on your hands this time?"

Jagger's voice softened to say, "Bobby's."

The big guy went numb.

"What?"

There'd been an accident outside the O, and police were on the scene. Onlookers gathered on the sidewalk to watch the two paramedics, Leslie and Jenny, tend to the injured victim on the road.

Matthew was out of the strip club. Seeing all the squad cars, he said to his top bouncer, "Virgil, what's going on?"

"The I-made-a-doodie guy got run over by a cop car."

Jenny said to Leslie, "Call it."

Leslie consulted his watch. He said, "Time of death: 9:05 PM."

The older man was now walking him to a bench, set in the long, gray walkway winding around eerie stone mausoleums and weathered headstones. They sat together.

"Listen, dingleberry—"

"Could you please not call me dingleberry?"

The older man said, "I know, I know," sympathizing with him. "This must be frightening for you. In time you'll get used to it. Right now it's all new to you."

"Exactly how *new* is this to me?"

"You've been worm food for almost four months."

Leslie said, in almost a whisper, "Four months."

"This is the fourteenth time I've had to stop you from reenacting the scene."

He looked at the old man.

"You were the stab victim. And it happened in a cemetery. *Greenwood* Cemetery."

"I came to lay flowers on my wife's grave," the older man said, "and now I'm lying beside her. Irony blows."

"Our delay must've killed you."

"*Must've*? I'm your neighbor. Another irony. So that makes you my responsibility." He raised his voice to the cemetery, "As much as I hate the job!"

"Who are you talking to?"

"You'll meet them."

Leslie said, "Did you say we were neighbors?"

"See for yourself."

Leslie looked in the direction of the older man's pointing decayed finger to a tombstone, the one planted near Paul St. George's. He got up from the bench and walked over. In the gloom of the night, the engraved stone could barely be read.

Leslie Case

1979–2015

Not much told there.

Leslie sighed. Still it was too big to swallow.

"Yep," he said. "That's me, all right."

What was it the old man said? In time he'll get used to it. Turning on his grave, he walked back to the bench . . .

Driving along now, half a block from the Fifth Avenue Market, he shuddered as a cold sensation rushed through his body.

Jenny said from the passenger seat, "What's wrong?"

Leslie glanced over. "Nothing. Somebody must've walked over my grave."

Then he saw an Alhambra heading toward them, and as he swerved to avoid it, they crashed and met their fate.

GUILT RIDDEN

It was 11:00 PM and it had been a long day. Dudley had until midnight before clocking out and going home. Sitting across the seat from him, Sadie Dallis-Price struggled to get her window open.

"There's something wrong with the window."

Dudley looked over at Sadie, Sadie wrestling with her window. Dudley looked in front of him at the traffic jam again, and said, "Might be because it's the only window closed."

"Could you open it?"

"I probably could, you know, if it wasn't stuck."

"It's jammed up good." Sadie pressed down on the window button a few more times before giving up. "You should get it fixed."

"Nah, best to leave it as it is." Dudley showing his irritation now. "You know, so that way you won't accidentally fall out."

The motorcycle screeched to a stop beside the Ford at Sadie's window. Dudley turned his head and saw the biker in the leather and helmet sit up straight on the seat, saw him reach in the leather jacket and bring out a .45 Caliber pistol—Dudley said, "Oh, shit," as the .45 was pointing at the passenger window, right where Sadie was sitting, and he had no time to think. The window exploded, showering them with glass. Sadie screamed and got a mouthful of shard glass. Dudley ducked under the steering wheel and threw his arms up to shield himself as bullets erupted into the body of the Ford in six, ten, thirty shots—and then it was over. The motorcycle sped away, leaving a ruined Ford in traffic.

Car alarms bursted in unison with chirping sounds. People screamed and a dog was barking.

No movement from the Ford.

Bobby's blood wasn't coming off. Jagger, stripped down to his underwear, was washing his scrubs in the toilet bowl of his prison cell. The saddest part wasn't that he was washing his only scrubs in the toilet. Worse, he'd be wearing it again.

Jagger raised the soaked scrubs to his nose, dripping toilet water, and sniffed it, recoiling. "Now it smells like toilet juice."

He needed to put it into a washer. The prison laundry service had those. No, then he'd have to explain the blood. There was another way, but it would require breaking his way out. Could he pull it off again, for the umpteenth time, without getting caught by the guards? He'd have to risk it.

Jagger stepped to the bars of his cell, quick, took one glance up and down the corridor to make sure no guards were nearby, then quietly retreated into the shadows of his cell.

The kitchen was big, about the size of a bowling alley. It had a commercial range and refrigerator, a long worktable in the middle of the room, and another table in the alcove of windows where the butler was clearing up. Bottles of gin, whiskey, rum, port, champagne, brandy, stout, and an ice tray were lined up on the worktable. Matthew was mixing a drink. The big guy looked up as Ray and Craig came in.

"Matt," Ray said, "we have to go if we want to beat all the sick people to the hospital."

Matthew said, "Did Bobby ask for us?"

Craig shook his head. "Hasn't come to since they put him in recovery."

"Give me a minute," Matthew said. He spiked the drink with a knockout drug.

Craig said, "What are you doing?" sounding shocked.

"I'm making a Hangman's Blood for Donald Trump."

Ray said, "You got Donald Trump in the house?"

Matthew nodded and Craig said, "You spiked Donald Trump's drink?"

"I have to close this deal by midnight," Matthew said, "and the man is being a stubborn-ass mule. This will bring him around. Now if you'll excuse me, I got to take Mr. Trump his medicine."

He walked out with Donald Trump's laced Hangman's Blood.

They arrived at Mount Sinai a little after two. Matthew and Craig came away from the nurses' station and were crossing the lobby to the elevators as Matthew said, "Had a meeting wit' the Japs today."

"How'd it go?"

"I tried to say erratic election," Matthew said. "And I almost made it."

Craig pushed the button for the elevator.

"What'd you wind up saying?"

Matthew said, "Not brassieres," and had to pause, looking around, one of them missing. "Where's Ray?"

"Do you mean where's Ray now, or where he will be in 2080?"

Craig nodded across the lobby to a good-looking nurse, on her break, talking to Ray. The nurse laughed at something Ray said. Ray flirting with the scrubs, looking to get laid tonight.

The elevator stopped on the fifth floor. Matthew called out to his friend, the Casanova, "Come on, Ray, we're going."

But his Irish friend, Craig, was louder, shouting to him, "Hey, Raymond, get your fucking bald head over here!" Getting disapproving looks from people in the lobby.

Matthew said, "Was that even necessary?"

"Sometimes yelling obscenities is the only way to land a bald eagle."

Ray called back, "You guys go on, I'll catch up. I'm finding out everything I need to know about the hot nurse."

Matthew walked up to them. He said, "Oh, is that what you're trying to do? Well, alright. Allow me." He said to the nurse, "Can you cook? He needs a woman who knows her way around the kitchen."

She said, "Um, no." Awkward, put on the spot.

"There," Matthew said to Ray. "Now you know everything you need to know." He went to the elevator as it opened and stepped in with Craig.

Ray was left with the nurse. He said to her, "Well …" kept looking at her and said, "See ya," and then walked off to catch the next elevator.

Bobby lay in the first bed of the semiprivate room, near the door, his eyes closed. There were tubes in his arms, one worming out of his nose, and another snaking from beneath the sheet to a catheter bag hooked to the bed.

Craig said, "Doctor said we shouldn't wake him."

"Fuck what the doctor said." Matthew put his hand on Bobby's shoulder and gave him a rough shake. "Get up, Bobby, Willie Nelson's brought some weed for you."

Craig watched Bobby's eyes roll open to see where Willie Nelson was with his weed before settling on them.

Bobby wasn't ready for them. He said, "Hey, guys …"

But then saw them staring at him with deadpan expressions.

Bobby kept his mouth shut.

He wanted to start again, try a little humor on them, maybe lightened the mood with, "I'm sure you're wondering why I gathered you all here today."

That didn't get a reaction either.

Jagger sat on the coffee table in his underwear. He was watching porn on the ninety-inch plasma TV. He said, "Everything on here is so big." Millicent came into the man cave, carrying a laundry basket of washed clothes, and Jagger quickly changed the channel and got more porn.

Millicent set the basket of laundry on the couch. "I wouldn't bother. You're not gonna find a decent thing to watch on that TV. All the channels are programed to porn."

"So all there is to watch is porn, porn, and more porn."

"Yeah. I wish that TV'd blow up."

"You know, Millicent," Jagger said, rising from the table, "if you want, I can get you a sledgehammer, and you could …" He mimed smashing the TV with an invisible sledgehammer.

"It doesn't bother me. I watch porn."

"Really?"

"Really."

"I had no idea girls watched porn."

"Well, you know the guys that the girls have sex with? Somebody's gotta cheer them on." She handed him his scrubs, washed and dried. "Okay, honey, your clothes are dry."

"Thanks."

Millicent watched Jagger in his underwear putting on the scrubs.

She said, "So you think Bobby's gonna be okay?"

"I hope so. I wanted to stay with him till the paramedics arrived, but I couldn't let anybody see me."

"The guys haven't called back from the hospital."

"Why didn't you go with them?"

"I had to do some packing. God, I hate packing."

"Why don't you hire some elves to pack for you? You could put your feet up and have 'em do all the heavy lifting. Totally up to you."

Millicent remembered something and laughed. "My mom once said people are short 'cause they carry too much heavy stuff on their head."

Jagger had his scrubs on, slipping an arm into the sleeve. He paused, sniffed the scrubs, and said, "I can still smell toilet juice."

Millicent said, "That's your breath."

There was an answer to that and he tried hard to think of what it was while she stood waiting to hear it. He opened his mouth to say it, ready to, but then his eyes went to the wooden plaque on the wall.

Now Millicent turned to follow his gaze, Jagger saying, "Hey, shit, the Ten Commandments plaque is filled up." Jagger looked over his shoulder at her. "Sorry, I meant to say 'The Ten *Man*ments.' " He smiled.

The guys' ten rules for the man cave were carved on a polished wooden plaque nailed to the wall of the man cave. The plaque read:

TEN MANMENTS

1. MAN MAKES RULES!
2. WOMEN MUST NOT ENTER MAN CAVE WITHOUT PERMISSION!
3. MAN DECIDES WHAT TO WATCH!
4. TOILET SEAT STAYS UP!
5. NO HIDING THE BEER!
6. FART, SCRATCH AND BELCH AT YOUR OWN FREE WILL!
7. NO FLOWER DECORATIONS!

8. TALK ABOUT *FEELINGS* MUST BE TAKEN OUTSIDE!
9. BITCHING BANNED!
10. NO QUESTIONING THE MAN CAVE RULES!

Jagger read, "'Women must not enter man cave without permission.'" And then looked at Millicent in the room.

"They don't like me coming in here all the time," Millicent said, "they should chop off my foot already."

The light on the answering machine was blinking.

Millicent brought it to attention. She said, "There's a message on the machine."

She edged to it, started to push the PLAY button and Jagger shouted, "Back away from the machine!"

He tapped on the Man Cave Rule plaque.

Millicent rolled her eyes, shaking her head. "Oh, right, the penis rule plaque."

There weren't many chairs around. Craig and Ray took the two by Bobby's bedside, and Matthew had to borrow one from the neighboring bed, whose occupant was snoring at three in the afternoon. Matthew lifted the chair and then brought it over and sat down. Now then … Matthew said, "Alright, young blood, start talking before I exchange your chart wit' Mr. Skelton"—reading the patient's chart—"who will be going in for triple bypass surgery at six."

Bobby said, "I found a bag of coke in the rest stop toilet and took it home."

Ray was eating Bobby's untouched lunch. He said, "You stole a bag of coke out of a crapper?"

Not what it sounded like. Bobby said, "No, I borrowed it for a couple hours."

"You throw the word borrow around so much," Matthew said, "it might as well be a virus."

"Well, excu-*u*-use me for learning a new word every day."

Craig told the idiot, "You've learned the same word for over a *month*."

They heard a sound, a ringing, coming from one of them. Craig and Ray searched themselves, then looked at Matthew.

"Matt?" Ray said. "You're ringing."

Matthew checked his watch for the time. He said, "It's Murphy." And let it ring.

"You're going to ignore the man who took you into his home and called you his son," Craig said, "when you came out of Africa with nothing but the Power Rangers knapsack on your back?"

"No, this is a much older and more spiteful version of that man."

"For the fifteen years since you ran away from home," Bobby said to his big brother, "you lived with this judge, and still I ain't met him."

"I didn't run away. The bus was leaving, and I caught it. I missed my stop and I never came back."

"Who was driving that bus? Freddy Krueger?"

"Don't try and change the subject after what you did."

"Funny, I thought I was staying on the subject."

"You really screwed up this one."

"I know, and I'm sorry." Bobby said, "But don't yell at me, aight?" his chin quivering, sad, putting it on. "I'm hurt."

"You should be more worried 'bout what'll happen when the long arm of the law gets to you."

"Nothing'll happen."

Craig said, "Bobby, you could go jail."

"I can plead insanity and get off with a slap on the balls. Hopefully by a young, hot she-judge."

"I don't think you realize the gravity of this situation," Matthew said. "You took Satan's dandruff out of the toilet, and it got an undercover cop killed. And now this cop killer is probably looking for his dandruff. What are you going to do when he finds out it was you who took it? Did you ever think of that?"

Bobby said, "I did not." He looked scared.

"You did not. And it took two lives."

Bobby said, "I know," and paused and said, "I don't wanna be here. How do I get out of it?"

"There's no getting out of this one, young blood. This is worse than the time you went into the pet store and taught all the parrots to swear."

"Maybe if I close my eyes, all my troubles will go." The fucking idiot closed his eyes, actually expecting it to work.

"Are they gone?" His eyes snapped open, something coming to mind. "Bro, you call Mom? Did you tell her her baby boy got shot?"

Matthew shook his head saying no. "I told her her son Bobby got shot."

"What'd she say?"

"She said she'll try and make it."

"She'll *try* and make it? But I'm her son."

Ray cleared it up for him. "Not her only son."

Craig said, "Kid, why don't you pack your needle and spoon, and book yourself a third-class ticket to South Africa and go see your mommy?"

"Does a corpse visit his relatives for its own funeral?"

Ray said, "If it's possessed, it would."

Bobby said, "I'd make the effort, except I got no money and no passport . . ." His voice trailed off as a cop walked in, a detective in a beige suit. "I mean—I got a passport, but it's expired. Please, don't report me to Immigration, Mr. Cop."

The cop's name was Yosef Olyphant, a rugged and outdoor kind of fella, and after introducing himself and showing his badge to Matthew, he suggested they take the discussion out in the hall. Olyphant invited Ray and Craig, saying he'd like to speak with them too.

Olyphant telling Matthew, "Your best friend broke out of prison, saved your brother's life, and then broke back in."

Matthew said, "Yeah …?" taking his time, then said, "And so, what's your point?"

Olyphant said, "I want to know how he's doing it."

"Look, Detective Elephant—"

"Olyphant."

Ray turned his head to Craig and muttered, "Rhymes with eggplant."

Matthew saying, "Jagger couldn't have been sitting at that diner wit' us. Because Jagger is living out the remainder of his pathetic, miserable life in prison without the possibility of parole."

"That's like banging your head on the wall," Craig said, "without ever stopping."

"I saw Jagger at the table with you," Olyphant said. "Everybody did."

Looking at the dick it was in Matthew's mind to give the impression Jagger meant nothing, the way to do it. Mind-fuck him, throw the dick off some. "You're sure everybody saw him," Matthew said, "or everybody saw you make an ass of yourself?"

"You're telling me you didn't *see* Jagger?"

Matthew believed it was working.

"We've been telling you for five minutes," Ray said.

"Whose turkey sandwich was it that I saw on the table?"

Craig said, "You were probably hungry and hallucinated the turkey sandwich."

Ray nodded, agreeing with him, then said, "Speaking of food," suddenly inspired, getting out his cell phone. Matthew asked if he was ordering take out. Ray said no, "I'm checking my messages. Why?"

While Yosef Olyphant stood with them slowly going crazy. "Are you saying that I've gone completely insane? I don't believe what I'm hearing."

Look at him. Oh yeah, he's confuckled.

Craig said, "Going batshit for thirty thousand a year doesn't seem worth it when you think about it, huh?"

"Thank you for your cooperation—waste of time!"

Olyphant walked off down the hall.

Ray said, "Well, that was a fun experience."

Half an hour remained of their session. Dr. Crowe was telling Dudley that it was never a good idea to bottle up his emotions inside. "One day you will explode," Dr. Crowe said. "You went through a very traumatic experience that took your wife's life."

Dudley lay on the couch and listened.

"You should let all your feelings of anger and guilt out."

Dudley's head turned this way to the shrink and a flare of anger filled his colorless, gray eyes.

Dr. Crowe recoiled from that malicious look, muttering rapidly to himself, "I take it back, I take it back, I take it back."

Dudley walked out of the nut room and saw Craig in the outer office talking to Dr. Crowe's assistant, Charlotte. Craig didn't see him. There were two other patients in the waiting area.

Craig said, "I'd like to see a shrink."

Charlotte said, "All right, what's wrong with you?"

Craig said, "I wish to wish the wish you wish to wish, but if you wish the wish the witch wishes, I won't wish the wish you wish to wish." She stared at him. "You got all that, right? 'Cause, you know, I don't like to repeat myself."

This was awkward. There was absolutely no way to get to the exit without passing Craig McCane, so he made himself known.

"Craig!"

Craig turned at the reception desk. "Hey, Dudley. How're you doing?"

"The shrink's office was the last place I expected to run into a familiar face."

"Nice to know you're as screwed up in the old noggin as the rest of the world. And how did it go with the brain shrinker?"

"You're kidding. That's what he was doing?"

Craig said, "That proves it—brains do shrink."

"What are you talking about? My brain's been the same size as always." Dudley adjusted his baseball cap, it was a little loose.

Craig said, "Have the cops found your wife's killer?"

"No, but I have."

"You found the shooter? Do the cops know this valuable piece of information?"

"Cops ain't getting their hands on this. No, I'm gonna handle it myself."

"Don't do anything foolish. You wouldn't want to wind up back here in a straitjacket."

"Speaking of straitjackets, what are you doing here?"

"I was supposed to receive my paycheck," Craig said. "It's been over a couple of weeks, and I still hadn't gotten paid. So naturally I went to talk to Ray to ask what's going on. Long story short, I plugged in the blender while he had his hand inside."

"I don't know whether that's bad timing or good timing."

"And now Matt's got me coming here once a week. He says I really could use a head doctor."

Dudley said, "You really could," and got ready to leave. "Well, listen, I have to get going if I want to be back here early next week." Walking off now. "Tell Raymond I said hey."

Craig said, "If I remember."

Coming outside, Dudley saw the Harley-Davidson motorcycle parked at the curb. He recognized it as the same one from the shooting.

The owner of the bike was returning to it, saw Dudley checking it out, and yelled, "Hey, you! Get away from my motorcycle!"

"Is this your motorcycle?"

The guy, clad in denim today, shoved Dudley away from the bike. With sarcasm in his voice he said, "Yeah—that's why I said get away from my hippopotamus."

"I've been looking for you."

The guy swung a leg over the seat and sat. "No time, got a list to complete."

"I know who you are."

"See ya."

The guy kicked the bike stand to get away, twisted the grip throttle and the motorcycle revved up. Dudley grabbed the front of the guy's jacket to keep him from speeding off.

"You're not listening to me," Dudley said, right in that stubbled face, "I know what you did, and if you don't want me going to the police you're gonna talk to me."

He pried Dudley's tight fingers off his jacket. "Get you're fucking hands off me."

Dudley was shoved. He staggered and came back, out of sorts. "It was you. Wasn't it? Yes it was. You're the fuck hole who did it."

The fuck-hole's name was Simon Cotton, and he pressed the muzzle of his caliber pistol to Dudley's belly, out of sight from people on the street.

Simon said, "I got a .45 pointed straight at your gut. There are snakes crawling around in my head, and when that happens, I shoot crazy. You don't want me blowing holes in you so far and wide, I suggest you *back off!*"

Dudley decided to lunge at him, regardless of what happened to him.

"Why you—" Dudley said, and a voice called to him on the street, saving him.

It was Millicent.

"Dudley? Oh my God, what are you doing?"

Dudley hesitated, then took off.

Millicent watched him hurry off and then turned to Simon. "Why was he putting his hands on you?"

"He thought I was a ham," Simon said. "Still want that coffee?"

"Yeah."

"Great, hop on. You're buying."

Dudley watched as the motorcycle putted away.

Millicent was packing her clothes into suitcases while Danny jumped on the white and gold canopy sultan's bed, a royal tent, the lush white curtains around the sides tied to the four posts with gold ribbons. The master bed.

Matthew kept to himself at the doorway, looking in the master bedroom at his daughter and his ex-wife, as he leaned against the doorframe.

Danny said, "Mommy, I wanna go with you."

"Sweetie—"

"I wanna go with you."

Millicent said, "Sweetie, no, you can't come with me."

"Why can't I come?"

"I'm going to see Grandma and Grandpa, but in the meantime, you're gonna stay here with Daddy, okay?"

Matthew would watch his daughter and her mother, the two of them together, and he'd start missing the way things were when they were a family. Matthew and Millicent would be in the Jacuzzi, and Danny would come and jump in, and they'd splash each other and have a good laugh. He still cared for Millicent. Wondered if she felt the same way. He had even looked into the possibility of reconciliation and weighed the pros and cons. The pros had always outweighed the cons. They had a good marriage, and it could still be good if they gave it another chance, worked hard at it. A possibility he'd been meaning to discuss with her. But it needed the right moment for that discussion, and this moment definitely wasn't right.

"I wanna go with," Danny said, her voice rising in a whiny tone, close to tears, but held. "I wanna go with you."

"Danny, stop jumping on the bed."

The sultan's bed that she was made in. Matthew, watching and smiling a little, remembered that day. Having coffee and then winding up at his place for sugar and cream, at one o'clock in the afternoon. Oh, he remembered it well.

Millicent had said, after sealing the deal, "How did you know I liked my coffee with cream?"

Now she was saying, "It's complicated," to their three-year-old daughter. "So I'm gonna try and explain this the best way I can, okay?" She said, "You can*not* come."

Danny zinged one in with, "Daddy's right—you're a bitch."

Matthew scrunched his face into an *ouch* expression. He could kiss reconciliation goodbye.

Millicent came toward him, a suitcase in each hand, and he knew he was going to get yelled at through clenched teeth.

"You tell her why she can't come with her Mommy."

She brushed past him in the doorway and Matthew felt himself shoved against the frame. She was surprisingly strong for a woman her size.

Matthew went after his ex-wife, to try and explain himself. Yeah, because that wasn't too late. Calling to her, "Millicent? Millicent?" She bound down the stairs. "Millicent, I didn't call you the B-word."

Jagger said, "Man, she looks sore as a baboon's ass."

He was at the staircase railing where it came up and curved into the open area of the hall, looking from Millicent to Matthew, Matthew saying, "Little advice? Never call your ex-wife a bitch in front of her child. Man, at this age kid's are like tape recorders."

Jagger was exposed at the top of the stairs, lit up like a green lantern.

Matthew snapped. "Jagger!"

The Redheaded Negro's shoulders jumped like a startled dog.

Jagger looked at Matthew saying, "Go back to prison before Olyphant announces a surprise cell inspection and figures out how you keep disappearing." He said, "He does, he's going to be on you."

"Like fly on shit," Jagger said. "Yeah, I know."

"*Jagger.*"

"All right, I'll go back to prison."

"Millicent?"

In the living room.

Millicent yelled at Matthew, "She's on the phone!" and went back to her phone call. "Hello? Yes, I'm still here. When will the cab get here?"

"I'll drive you to the airport," Matthew said. They could talk in the Rolls-Royce. She was more at ease and agreeable in the Rolls-Royce.

"Okay. And please, tell the driver to *hurry.*"

Matthew sighed, alright. "I'll pay the fare."

"Ah, well, you can tell the driver to wait outside and keep the meter running," Millicent said. "Money is no object."

Matthew grunted. You try to be generous.

Millicent was off the phone now.

"That takes care of that."

Matthew said, "And who takes care of these boxes?"

She looked at them. "Oh, right."

"Millicent, it has been a month since you've moved out. I beg you, woman, take your boxes wit' you."

"I was gonna put them in storage," Millicent said, "but I got my clothes and that's all I'm gonna need. The rest of my stuff you can just turn 'em into a bonfire. What the hell, go crazy."

Matthew said, "I didn't tell Danny you're a bitch."

Millicent caught Matthew's eyes move to glance at Jagger, Jagger watching TV, not looking this way, doing a damn good job of staying out of it.

She said, "Uh-huh," not buying it, "and where do you supposed she picked up the word?"

"I didn't think she was listening."

Jagger kept staring at the TV.

"I'm not surprised you'd put that word in my daughter's head. That's how you've always been, made me out to be the bad guy. Like in court. The lies you boasted about me being a bad influence on our child. God, I hate you for that."

"They weren't lies," Matthew said. "Just deep moving stories."

Jagger snuck a look at them, Millicent saying, "You honestly believe you can do a better job of raising her than her own mother?"

Matthew threw at her, "You mean the mother who told her child to start fights?"

Jagger wished Matthew would shut up.

"I don't tell her to start fights," Millicent said. "I tell her to *finish* them."

"Oh, she finishes them, alright. She put the ten-year-old paperboy in a body cast."

"He started it. And she finished it."

She shrugged her shoulders saying it, like it wasn't a big thing. Her response just made it that much easier for Matthew to say, "Danny will be better off wit' me."

"I'll get you back for this, Matthew. There is no way I'm gonna let you take my child from me. No way." She turned on her heels. Walking out she yelled, "No way!"

Matthew yelling after her, "I already have!"

He turned, Jagger looking at him now, shaking his head.

"Very mature."

Matthew was already regretting it. He said, "I used to be mad crazy 'bout that girl. I'd find myself at that Inn she worked at, watching her and wanting to hold her. *Hold her*—shoot, eat her out. The fact that she was almost illegal held me back from doing anything stupid that'll wind me in jail. I lost that fight."

Jagger nodded, following.

"I made the first move and talked to her, introduced myself, and then hearing her say my name, *Matthew*, I told myself, 'Man, I am fucked.'"

Jagger smiled. "She got you."

"She got me. From then on I couldn't keep her out of my dreams, woke up in sweat and wit' a raging boner." Matthew said, "And now she's packed and walking out of my life. What happened, Jagger?"

Jagger took time to think about it, but all he said was, "Time slipped away."

Bobby told his big brother, the former undisputed heavyweight champion boxer, that two cops dropped by the hospital to question him and he damn near wet his draws. All Matthew wanted to know, "What'd they ask you?" Everything but what he wore to bed at night, Bobby said, they made it sound like he was asking to get shot, and then said, blubbering, "Man, cops know just what to say to make a drug addict cry."

Matthew took them back to a few years ago. He said, "Remember when we found each other?"

Remember? Shit.

Bobby smiled, saying, "I can still taste the .44 Magnum barrel in my mouth." Meaning when he had been homeless and rooting through garbage for food and clothing.

He had made a hell of a racket. Matthew had been sitting in a Bentley parked at the curb, closely watching a house that wasn't his. He heard the homeless guy eating noisily from a garbage in an alley and lowered the driver's window to yell at him, "Keep the noise down, will you? I'm on eagle eye here!" The rummaging continued. "If you don't stop, I'm going to come over there and make you!" This time the rummaging did stop, but not for long, a few moments, and then it started up again. Matthew drew the .44 Magnum from the compartment in the dashboard, his hands in brown leather gloves, and made for the noise in the alley. He took a handful of the homeless guy's hair, yanked his head back and saw that he was just a kid. The scavenger was a boy in his late teens, on his own, and homeless, the boy yelling, "Hey, shit, let go of me," looking into Matthew's face as he took in a mouthful of Magnum. Matthew had said to him that time, "Listen, you worthless piece of shit, I 'bout had enough of you. You make one more noise, I'll shoot you." While the homeless boy gagged on six pounds of steel. "You don't know me yet, you're 'bout to." The boy got a proper look at him, the revolver shoved down his throat. His glazed eyes widened, recognizing familiar features of himself in him. He made a sound around the Magnum. Matthew pulled six inches of barrel out of the boy's mouth, and the boy said, "Matt? Jesus Christ, is it really you?" Matthew wanted to know who the fuck he was. "Matt, it's me. Don't tell me you don't recognize me." Matthew squinted at the homeless kid, studied him, and his face softened as he said his little brother's name for the first time

those African kids that he saw them as his own. "They're super great kids, I hate losing them."

He turned and was gone before Slowpoke said, "Think that's the only rich guy to ever talk to me I ain't robbed."

"Nobody cares," Bobby said. "What's going on, Slowpoke? What'd you wanna tell me?"

He could see Slowpoke was going to sit down. There were three chairs in the room, Slowpoke chose neither, instead he chose to sit on the bed, his fucking butt aiming for the catheter and Bobby had to move the tube quick.

"Watch where you park that thing!"

"My bad," Slowpoke said, and got to it. "The kingpin whose dandruff you took from the toilet? He's going around asking about you. He's vowed to wipe out every living soul in the Bronx 'less his dandruff is returned."

"Who is this Michael Myers wannabe?"

"Got no fucking clue," Slowpoke said. "But I do know, he's only got one hand he eats and wipes his ass with." He then said, "Aight," with no more to report. "Where's the slice of pizza you promised me?"

"Huh?"

"You called, you said you had an extra slice of pizza."

"That was two days ago."

"I'll heat it up in the microwave," Slowpoke said. "Now, come on, where's my slice of pizza?"

Bobby, frowning hard, told him, "Floating in the Bronx River with the rest of my Friday night dinner."

Millicent looked at the newborn babies through the window of the hospital nursery. Matthew walked up. She watched him pretend to look around, Matthew saying, "Can't find your way out of here either, huh?"

Millicent said, "I was welcoming the newborn," and to the newborns, "Welcome to our world. It's cruel. It's corrupt. You'll fit right in." She said, "Look at them, so fresh out of the oven and looking scrumptious."

"Mind if I look wit' you?"

"Yes, I do mind. But that's me doing you."

"Man, I am such a dick."

There was a silence, both of them admiring the babies in their incubators. Now Millicent turned her head to look at Matthew.

"You find out who told the cops Bobby stole the coke?"

Matthew said, "Not yet," and looked at her, into those hazel eyes that moved and gleamed, reflecting the hall's fluorescent lights. "Do you know something? Since you always know everything."

"Well, you know, it helps if you play dumb. I'm so good at playing dumb, the son of a bitch I married actually thinks I'm dumb, and takes my child from me."

"I didn't take her from you because you're dumb."

Millicent turned on him. "You think I'm dumb?"

"I—uh—no, I don't think you're dumb."

"That's right," Millicent said, "and I can take care of my child."

"I know you can."

"So give her *back* to me, damn it. I keep asking you to let me see her, but no, you're afraid I'm gonna leave her on the subway. That happened *one* time. And that was only because the only guy in the speedo distracted me." She looked into the nursery, giving herself time to calm down. "Ever loved somebody so much you could die for them?"

Matthew couldn't keep his eyes off her.

She said, "Big Boy?"

It brought Matthew back. He felt that familiar stir he got whenever he was around her.

"What?"

She was smiling at the babies. "They're the most beautiful creatures in the world."

Matthew, gazing at her, so smitten, said, "You most definitely are."

"What?"

He turned his head to the nursery. "Yes, the babies are beautiful."

Damn.

Ray was firing the grizzled janitor. He wished he knew the guy's name so he could throw it in while he worked up to it. He started off with, "Your work at the club has been appreciated, but we no longer appreciate you."

The janitor said, "What does this mean?"

Ray stopped pacing. He said, "If we've got do this the hard way …" Ray sat down and hunched over the desk, looked at the janitor and finished with, "You're fired."

"Who's gonna replace me?"

Goddammit, what was his name. He knew it was Nick something. Ray had it at the tip of his tongue and then lost it as he was saying, "I don't know who's going to replace you, and I don't care. Everybody who works here don't like you. Now go away."

With nothing further to discuss, the janitor heaved himself up from the chair to go.

"And while you're on a roll," Ray said, "you may want to change your name."

The janitor turned at the door. "What's wrong with Nicodemus?"

"*Ni*codemus! That's it."

The janitor walked out of the office, with his tail between his legs.

Craig came in a moment later and asked, "Want to go outside for a smoke?"

"Why," Ray said, "is Lauryn Hill outside?"

"I wanted to talk to you about Dudley."

"You can talk to me in here. I've removed all the bugs."

"You've bugged the office with listening devices?"

Ray gave him a look. "Who said anything about *listening* devices?"

"Do you want to know what Dudley's planning to do, or make faces?"

"Tell me," Ray said. Craig told him. "Jesus Christ, Dudley is going after the killer?"

"The man is out of his mind."

"Well, what's he doing out of his mind? He should get back in there." Ray stared off into space as he said, "Most of the time I'm in my mind, get away from the world, chill out with Lauryn Hill. I may dim the lights a little. I never, *ever*, turn the lights all the way out." Shaking his head. "Oh, nooo."

"All right, Raymond, come on out of your head."

Ray blinked and looked at Craig, as though he'd forgotten who he was.

"Yes, can I help you?"

She was in a private room. Dudley stood at the bed saying, "Why did he try to kill you?"

"Kill me? I thought he was aiming for you and missed. I was only in front because the backseat made me carsick. I don't know why a biker would want to kill me. All I know is that he tried and failed. I'm still alive. Well, barely."

Dudley said, "Somebody hired this guy to kill you." He watched her eyes move to the door as her husband arrived, a man in a dark toupée carrying a bouquet of pink lilies.

She tried on a smile. "James."

James approached the bed saying, "Sadie," Dudley catching the note of surprise in his voice. James saw him. "Who are you?"

"I'm Dudley. I was with your wife on the day of the shooting."

"So you're the one who brought her to the hospital."

"And he was just leaving," Sadie said.

Dudley got the hint. Before he could excuse himself James said, "Thank you very much," with bitter disappointment, Dudley wasn't sure. "If you hadn't brought my wife in when you did, I'd be preparing for her funeral by now."

Dudley said, "It was nice to meet you folks," and got the hell out of there.

Outside, getting in the driver's seat of the taxicab, Dudley said, "Sorry I kept you waiting."

His passenger glared at him from the backseat.

Dudley said, "Where to?"

A moment later the taxicab with the bullet holes, pulled out of the parking space and drove its passenger into traffic.

They sat with Dudley in Cookie's coffee shop on West Thirty-fifth Street. Dudley said, "I plan on meeting this guy, but not in the way you think."

The waitress brought their coffee and chocolate chip muffins.

Ray said, "Muffins are here," and took them from her.

Craig looked directly at Dudley saying, "Whatever you're thinking to do? Forget it, all right?"

Ray raised his muffin to take a bite and pause. "Okay, but I don't see how else I can eat this muffin."

"With any luck, the guy won't show up," Craig said, and the guy did, walked in to Cookie's like anybody was welcome.

Dudley motioned to him. "Hey."

Ray leaned on the arm of his chair, close to Craig. "He showed up."

Dudley looked at them. He said, "Stay …" Getting up from the table. "And save me a muffin."

The second Dudley walked off to talk to Simon, Ray said, "Find it," and began looking under the table and chairs.

Craig, going along, looking around, said, "What are you looking for?"

"Chainsaw, machete. Something he might've taped under the table. Basically, anything liable to slice a human being in half."

Craig held a rat by the tail. "What about this rat?"

Ray turned his head, said, "No," and kept looking.

Craig released the rat. "Go on with what you were doing, little fella."

Dudley handed Simon a photograph.

Simon looked it over and immediately frowned. He said, "This is the guy?"

Dudley nodded.

"Are you kidding me?"

To show he was serious, Dudley produced a thick envelope.

Craig watched the money exchange. "You know what I've been thinking?"

"I don't care what you've been thinking," Ray said, in a tone that got Craig's attention.

"What's with you?"

"You talk like you know, but just don't care." In a bad mood all of a sudden.

"Is this about me plugging in the blender too soon?"

"'Cause of you, I am a man short of a finger."

Craig said, "Your victory sign is going to look all weird, huh?" He smiled, but Ray didn't. "Look, man, I said I was sorry."

"Oh, you're sorry. That makes everything okay. Oh, wait. No, it doesn't."

Dudley returned to the table and Craig asked him, "Where can I find a prosthetic middle finger?"

Dudley said, "In the belly of a shark."

Ray said, "Didn't you say you were going to get the guy that killed your wife?"

Dudley said, "I am."

Craig nodded to the door to Cookie's coffee shop. "Wasn't that the guy that killed your wife?"

"No, he's a hit man."

Something else was going on, Craig could feel it, but wasn't sure what exactly. He said, "What was in the envelope?"

"More to the point," Ray said, "whose photo did you give him?"

"The person who is responsible for all my suffering and burdens," Dudley said. "The one that killed my Abbey."

Ray said, "And who does the honor go to?"

They heard the blast of the large caliber revolver and the sound of the coffee shop window glass shattering. They saw the blood appear on the chest of the light-colored shirt, a grunt from Dudley, the wind knocked out of him, then saw more blood appear on the shirt as Simon fired some more shots through the broken plate glass. Dudley fell onto the table, his face plunged into Ray's chocolate chip muffin. People screamed and dashed out of the way. A coffee cup exploded in a man's hand. There was an outburst of people shouting "Shots!" and "Everybody get down!"

It soon settled down. The shots ceased and Simon vacated the scene, his target terminated. Craig and Ray came up from under the table and sat there like they were afraid to move.

"Ray, this is the second time a man's dropped dead on our table," Craig said. "Are you as scared as I am?"

"There's a dead guy in my muffin," Ray said, "I'm fucking terrified."

They were still looking at the newborn babies. Matthew turned to her. "Listen, Millicent? I had a talk wit' my lawyer and—" He reconsidered. "No, you don't want to hear this."

She said, "I do."

He smiled at her. "You said the same thing on our wedding day. Exactly like that." He cleared his throat. "Look, I realized I'm being unreasonable by keeping Danny from you. But understand—I was angry. I kept her mainly to hurt you. Like you hurt me when you slept wit' my best man."

"Oh."

"Don't think you're a bad mother. You're not. I'm the one got issues. But I'm over 'em now."

"So I can see Danny?"

Matthew said, "What if I say we could work something out?"

She turned enough to look at him, smiling, that gleam in her eyes.

"I'd say 'Keep talking, Big Boy.' " She'd call him that in bed and he'd call her Mama as they reached that volcanic love eruption.

It gave him the feeling they were becoming close and he liked it and if she was putting it on, playing him, so what.

She said, "What is it?"

Matthew felt a tenderness. "I was thinking 'bout our first date." He waited a couple beats and said, "That night?"

She made a sound "Ohhh," nodding, calling the night to mind.

"Remember?"

"Uh-huh."

"Wild."

"Mm."

"We must've done it, like, four times."

"Five."

"Five? Jesus, we were animals."

"Out of control."

There was a silence.

Matthew said, "Well, you know, sex wit' you was always incredible."

She had to agree. She said, "It was." With pride.

"So incredible," Matthew said. "I got to your place, took one look at you in that tight little number and jumped you." He said, "No part of you escaped me that night." He said, "Yeah, that wasn't very gentleman of me, was it?"

"From my place, to the restaurant and back to your place, we must've done it a lot. I mean every chance we got."

Silence again.

Matthew said, "It probably helped that I lived so far away."

"It helped a lot."

Matthew and Millicent looked longingly at each other.

Jagger, in shackles behind a panel of bulletproof glass, sat across from Yosef Olyphant.

"One man was poisoned, and another was shot," Olyphant said. "Your fingerprints were at the scene of the crime, Jagger. We found them on the dials of the apartment telephone used to make the 911 call."

Jagger toyed with his bracelets. "Detective, I've been inside five years for mutilating my dear mother. I ain't been no place else. Trust me."

"No two people have matching fingerprints."

"Have you fingerprinted everyone on the planet to verify your theory, Detective?"

They were wasting time. Olyphant said, "Come on, Jagger. How can you be in two places at once?"

Jagger fingered the left handcuff. The ring of the cuff popped open.

Olyphant felt a start in him. "What are you doing?"

Jagger said, "I'm not doing anything."

He snapped the cuff ring closed. Then popped it open. Now the cuff ring was open, now the cuff was closed.

It was open; it was closed.

Olyphant's eyes stayed on that cuff ring.

Jagger began to work on the right cuff ring like a magician doing a trick. He took off both cuffs and then snapped them back on.

Olyphant yelled, "Guard!" A guard came over. "Are those cuffs locked?"

The guard inspected Jagger's shackles.

He said, after, "They're locked."

Jagger waited, the guard moved off before he spoke.

"Like I said, Detective Olyphant, there's no possible way for me to be in two places at once."

Ray and Craig watched with the crowd on the sidewalk as police investigators examined Dudley's body in the coffee shop, a total crime scene.

Craig said, "I wasn't aware Dudley was having problems. I mean, living with the guilt of killing your own wife. You know? I should've known something was wrong when I ran into him at my shrink's office. I guess we only see what we want to see, huh?"

Ray stared at the crime scene another few moments before saying, "I'm not going to finish that muffin, am I?"

BEHIND BARS

They were discussing drugs. Millicent, seated two chairs from Matthew, said, "I don't understand. Is it so hard to say no to drugs?"

"No, it's not," Ray said. "But what do I know, eh?"

Craig said to him, "Nothing." He sat between Matthew and Millicent. Since they divorced, they were always at each other's throats, and Craig positioned himself there intentionally to keep the fights to a minimum.

"Only an idiot would get himself hooked," Millicent said.

"Yes," Craig said, "and only Bobby would get shot over it."

Ray said, "That's 'cause Bobby's an idiot."

"Come on, guys," Matthew said, "that's my little brother you're talking 'bout."

Millicent said, "The idiot."

"Yes," Matthew said. He was looking at Millicent. She was wearing the knitted sweater dress he liked, crotch-high and tight around her curves. Her slim, tanned legs were crossed. She glanced at him. He smiled, and she looked away.

Ray was saying, "Doesn't Bobby know that drugs bring trouble into the home? It's like slutty high school girls getting knocked up."

Millicent scoffed. "Yeah, that's exactly what it's like, high school girls growing marijuana in their tiny bellies."

She looked at Matthew again, Matthew staring at those hazel eyes gleaming, taking her beauty in. She turned her head before he could see what was in her eyes.

"I guess Bobby can't help being stupid and weak and selfish," Ray said. "Drugs have really messed him up."

Craig said, "Nothing more pathetic than a drug addict."

"God, Bobby's an idiot."

"Such an idiot."

Talking about him while he was in the bed. Bobby said, "Guys, I'm in the room!"

Yosef Olyphant stood with Jagger in the corridor, while Bostick scrutinized Jagger's cell for an escape tunnel.

Jagger said, "What's Taz-Mania doing in there?"

Olyphant said, "Making a right mess of the place, looks like."

"Don't you just hate it when a white man goes through a nigga's junk?"

"No."

"Uh-huh," Jagger said. "Well, that's 'cause you've always been the white man. I go through this shit every day." He said, "It's the best feeling ever!"

Olyphant said, "Jagger, I don't give a shit about you, not when you're inside. When you're in here, you're not my problem. You're their problem. It's when you're outside that I start cussing and fussing."

Jagger said, "Detective Olyphant, I'm gonna say it again." And said it. "I haven't been anywhere beyond these walls."

"You're getting out somehow."

Bostick made a hell of a racket in Jagger's cell which got Jagger yelling at him, "Hey, hey, hey! How'd you feel if I made a mess in your house?"

Bostick said from the cell, "Like a nigga."

He gave up and came out, a well-bred law dog from the city.

Olyphant said, "Well, partner, what'd you find?"

"Diddly-squat."

Olyphant looked at him deadpan.

Bostick said, "No tunnel."

Bobby said to Craig's delicate wife Joanna, "You won't believe what I'm wearing under this hospital gown."

Joanna tried to avoid eye contact with him; her face lacked makeup, her features washed-out beneath a slight pregnant lady glow.

Craig showed the guys a picture of his new sports car. "Get a load of this beauty."

They oohed and ahhed.

"I call her Godzilla."

Joanna, eight-months-pregnant, said, "I call her 'an accident waiting to happen.'"

"I'm telling you, this baby is fast. It's reliable, and it doesn't melt in the sun."

Ray said, "Your last car, Craig—was it built by snowmen?"

Joanna said, "Could someone ask him how much this piece of crap cost?"

Bobby did. "Yo, Craig, how much did this piece of crap cost?"

"Money, schmoney."

"You see?" Joanna said. "Same response every time." She got up, holding her baby bump. "All right, I have to go see my mom. Anybody want to give a pregnant girl a ride?"

"No problem, babe," Craig said. "I'll drive you anywhere you want to go."

"Can you take me back to last week when the car was at the dealership?"

"What's the matter? You don't like my car?"

She said, "No, no, I like it, I do. It's just …" She paused to think up a good lie. She said, "Matt promised to drive me. Didn't you, Matt?"

He saw what she was getting at. Matthew said, "See, this is why I don't make promises. I forget I make 'em."

"Take me to my mom's?"

They watched Matthew and Joanna walk out into the hall, Matthew picking up Joanna's coat from the chair and putting it over her shoulders.

Craig said, his gaze following them, "But the car's all juiced up to go."

Ray said, "Don't you have work to do?"

"Oh, man," Craig said, "my job takes up all my fun time."

Matthew was in his home office, in a meeting with his corporate lawyer, Amir Jo. This room was his business room, it had a picture window behind a large oak desk with two telephones. He had a black one for personal calls and the red one he made his millions on, managing his long line of businesses. Today wasn't about business. Anytime they weren't talking business, they kept to the living room area and helped themselves to hooch from the minibar. When the drinks were poured, they stretched out in comfortable leather chairs in front of the glass coffee table and watched the stock market on the large TV.

Amir said, "You signed your divorce papers uncontested?"

Matthew sipped his Scotch. "Yeah, this way neither of us wastes money on lawyers, and it'll save a lot of bloodshed."

"Does this mean shared custody of Danny?"

Matthew nodded. "Along wit' thousands of dollars in alimony."

"And this is really what you want?"

"No," Matthew said, with a buzz from the Scotch. "What I really want is a longer weekend, a glass of bubbly, hot tub, and the love of my life using me as a human-powered transport to get me from point A to B. But we can't always get what we want."

Amir noticed Millicent in the doorway. He sat up in the leather chair and said, "Speak of the devil."

Matthew said, "That's no devil. That's my ex-wife."

"Yeah …?"

"How 'bout you don't talk while she's here?"

"I can do that."

Matthew said, "Alright, well, just do your best." Matthew looked at Millicent now. "Come on in."

She came into the lamplight, and Amir saw her face, cut and bruised.

"W-ouch."

Matthew saw her clearly then, as he was about to take another sip of his drink. He said, "Jesus Christ," lowering his glass. "Don't tell me you were in a—"

"Fight club," Millicent said, and said to him, "Listen, could you take Danny today?"

Matthew hesitated. "Alright, sure, I can do that."

"I promise this is gonna be the last time."

"She was looking forward to spending some time wit' you, Millicent. She couldn't stop talking 'bout it. Man, she'll be disappointed."

She did this all the time and it about drove Matthew insane. She could never seem to find time for Danny. She always left Danny with him and went off to do her own activities.

She said, as she always did, "Please, take her?"

He hesitated again.

"Fine."

Millicent said, "Tell her I'll make it up to her," and walked out.

Amir called after her, "Good-bye, Millicent." He didn't get a response. "Nothing. She's the only woman in the world who intimidates me."

Matthew went to the minibar and topped up his glass. "Probably 'cause she's the only one who can beat you up."

"She's still fighting."

"I'll never get use to those bruises."

Amir said, "Speaking of potential dangers, have you ever wondered what it'll be like to stick your foot inside a bear trap?"

Matthew came and sat down saying, "You've asked scarier questions. Wait. Was it you who put the bear trap in my brother's hospital room?"

"As your corporate lawyer, Matt, I care about your health."

Matthew raised his glass to his mouth saying, "Good. 'Cause my doctor couldn't give a shit."

He sipped his Scotch.

Amir said, "Well, unlike your doctor, I give a shit."

"We all give a shit, Amir. Anyway," Matthew said, "why this sudden interest in my medical records?"

"Accidents happen."

"Yeah, and apparently not often to you lawyers."

Matthew's cell phone chirped.

Amir said, "Don't answer. It could be your foster father."

Matthew checked the caller ID and said, "It's not. It's the Irish Whiskey."

And answered the call.

"McCane."

"Matt."

"Where are you?"

"I'm outside."

"So come inside."

"Actually, can you come outside?"

Matthew said, "But it's warmer inside," gave in, saying, "Alright," hung up, then called out, "Ray?" Ray was in the bathroom taking a dump, Matthew telling him, "Craig wants us outside."

The office toilet flushed. Coming out and fastening the belt of his pants Ray said, "He got into an accident?"

Amir looked up at Ray standing by his recliner. "Why would you wish a thing like that on your best friend?"

Ray gave the Japanese lawyer a look that was deadpan. "It was my last wish and I made it."

They walked out to the front porch and saw Craig looking over his McLaren, the car totaled. Matthew said, "Jesus Christ," and Ray asked, "Is that your McLaren?"

Craig had to look at it again and then nod his head in confirmation. He said, "I don't know what happened. I'm coming over, driving my brand-new sports car and this rustbucket crashed into me."

Craig was a fast driver, loved the rush, the thrill. It was why he loved driving at night, so he could run through red lights.

Matthew said, "How fast were you driving?"

Craig turned his back to the wrecked sports car. Easier to lie that way.

"I wasn't driving that fast."

"How fast?"

Craig shrugged, it was a small movement, a gesture of no importance. "Sixty, eighty … hundred and twenty. I don't know," Craig said, "The needle kept going up and up."

Ray said, "Jesus Christ, man, did you think to slow down when you saw the needle go up to a hundred?"

"The fuck would I want to slow down for?"

Matthew said, "For the very reason your McLaren is now totaled."

"I'm alive, aren't I?"

Amir Jo told him yes, he was alive. He said, "This time you caught a big break," and watched Craig frown at him.

"There's nothing wrong with wanting to drive a little over the speed limit."

Ray said, "Say that again with a straight face."

At the Piars mansion later in the evening, Ray brought Joanna McCane to see the wreck. Craig had the McLaren in the garage and was emptying the glove box. He didn't hear them come in.

He didn't know they were in the hall that led to the garage until Ray said, "Craig, look who's visiting?"

Craig came out of the McLaren to see Ray, saw Joanna and his stomach took a plummet.

Craig said, "*Ray*," hissing it at him, "of all the people you could've brought—Osama Bin Ladin, Adolf Hitler, Lucifer. Why'd you bring my *wife*?"

"They're all dead and she's pregnant and *breathing*." Ray said, "The hormones are going crazy, people! The mood swings are active!" with a charge, then stood back and watched, grinning.

Joanna said, "I had to see this for myself."

Craig took her arm and brought her into the garage. "Now, babe, I got to warn you. It's not a pretty sight. Know there was nothing I could've done to prevent this—"

"You could've driven slow," Ray said.

Craig glared at him and then said to Joanna, "The good news is that I'm alive to give you many more years of nookie."

Then she saw the wreck. Joanna saying, "Oh, my God!"

"I know, it looks really bad, doesn't it?"

"I can't believe what I'm seeing." Joanna started to well up, overjoyed. "This was so meant to be!"

He looked at her. "Say what, now?"

"Oh, no, real tragedy about your midlife crisis. But I am just so happy!"

Craig was touched. He took his radiant pregnant wife into his arms. "Aw, you're happy your hubby is alive?"

"No! I'm surprised you're alive! Just look what you walked *away* from!"

Craig, Ray and Bobby crowded into the doorway of Bobby's hospital room to watch several physicians work furiously on a patient across the hall.

Craig said, "Ten bucks says he's going to make it."

"The guy's life is hanging in the balance," Ray said, "and you're making money off it? How insensitive can you get?"

The physicians seemed to be failing to revive the patient.

"We're losing him!"

Ray said, "Make that twenty."

The patient's machine ran a flat line.

Craig said, "Aaand he's gone."

Bobby grumbled, "Lucky bastard."

Craig dug a fifty out of his pocket. "You got change for a fifty?"

Ray snatched the fifty and made it disappear. "I'll get back to you on that."

They returned to Bobby's room, Bobby climbing into bed. Craig spotted something under the bed.

"Fuck me Freddie." Craig held up a bear trap. "What's this bear trap doing in here?"

Bobby said he didn't know, he woke up this morning and it was there.

"Matt warned me we might find a bear trap planted in the room," Ray said, and looked at Bobby. "Gift from his corporate lawyer."

"The Japanese brief?" Craig said.

"I didn't know Amir was Japanese," Bobby said. It got them frowning at him, couldn't understand how he could've missed it, and he said, "Thought he was *Chi*nese."

He started playing with the machines. Craig told him they weren't for playing.

"Why? What would happened if I did?"

Ray gave him a slap upside the head. He said, "That."

"Listen, guys," Bobby said. "I appreciate you coming to see me, but I'd like to be alone now, please."

Ray said, "Who're you kidding?" and took a seat.

Millicent appeared with a newspaper in hand she had folded to the apartment listings, a few possibilities crossed out in a green marker. She said to someone on the phone, "Well, thank you anyway," and hung up. "Stuck-up bitch."

Seeing her, Bobby's whole mood lit up. He liked Millicent. The two were very close. She was like a sister to him, and in hard times she became like a mother, both in their early to mid-twenties. Or perhaps because Millicent was the only one who took the junkie in when everybody else gave up on him.

Smiling at her now, Bobby said, "Hey, Mill." As she approached, he saw her bruised face. Millicent smothered him with kisses. When she let him breathe, he said, "Looks like you just won a fight."

Millicent said, "I have." She sat close to Bobby on the bed, then put an arm around him and said, "I can't find a decent apartment in this city, though. The ones I've seen either belonged to a dead guy or used to be a crack house."

Craig said, "There's a bum in the alley looking to sell his cardboard box, if you're interested."

"Do you really wanna get on my ugly side?"

Ray said, "Looks to me like someone already has."

Bobby took the paper from her. "You look at every apartment on here?"

Millicent nodded. "None of them are any good. And three-bedroom houses cost more."

Ray said, "How much do you get fighting?"

"I can make two grand in one night."

Bobby said to Millicent, "Your bookie don't mind you making money on the side?"

"Not unless he doesn't know."

"He'll kill you he finds out you been betting on yourself?"

Millicent said, "Soldier, I'm in a tight spot for cash. Last girl I grappled with cost me five grand."

Ray could see why Matthew married her. Millicent was beautiful, street-wise, and easy to talk to. She was a female version of the Champ.

She watched Bobby picking lint off his shoes. "I think it's dirty, Bob."

Craig got up, said he had to go pick up Jo from her mother's.

Millicent made a face. "Ooh."

"What?"

"Joanna kinda asked me to pick her up."

"She asked you?"

Ray said, "And I drove her to the grocery store earlier this afternoon."

"Also she asked me to drop her off at her nail salon," Bobby said, "and I would've, if I had a car and wasn't stuck in this hospital with my butt imprinted on the bed."

"So she asked me instead," Ray said. Craig asked what's going on. "Nothing, it's just that ..." Ray did his best to find the right words. "Jo hates your driving. Yeah, she says you drive too fast."

"Like a madman," Millicent said.

"I believe her exact words were 'Like the Devil after a bottle of Hennessy.'"

Bobby drew his knees up and swung around to get out of bed saying, "And after your accident the other night …"

Millicent said, "We kinda understand where she's coming from."

Craig said, "You guys don't think I drive like a devil on a drunken night out, do you?"

Ray said, "Yeah," and Bobby said, "We do."

"I see."

Millicent watched him. "Do you?"

"Hell no, I don't see!"

Millicent said to Ray, "No, he doesn't see," her gaze followed Bobby as he wheeled his IV pole with him to the lavatory. He opened the door to go in.

"There's the toilet!" Bobby looked at his friends. "And all this time I been peeing in the plant pot."

He walked into the lavatory. The others looked toward the bamboo plant. It was dead.

She stopped a nurse and asked, "Excuse me? Can these Styrofoam cups be taken outside?"

The nurse told Millicent to do whatever she wanted with them.

Millicent said, "Oh-kay." And she turned, bumped into Matthew, and dropped her paper. She said, "Matthew," surprised to see him. "Hi."

"Hey," Matthew said. He picked up her paper and saw the apartment listings, most of them crossed out. "Your paper."

"Thanks."

"How's my knucklehead brother doing?"

"Up and about." She felt awkward around him. "Craig and Ray are with him now. But I'll see you later."

Matthew saw her eyes for a moment with a look he remembered and then she turned and headed for the exit.

"Millicent?"

She turned back around.

"Yeah?"

"Are you alright?"

"I'm fine."

That silence.

She said, "Okay, this was fun."

Millicent got two steps toward the automatic doors and Matthew stopped her.

"Wait."

Millicent spun around. She said, "If you haven't already caught on, Matthew," with a note of exasperation, "I'm kind of in a hurry to get away from you, so …"

"Millicent," Matthew said, "just because we don't shower together anymore doesn't mean we can't be comfortable around each other."

"I'm comfortable around me. Aren't you?"

He gave her his serious stare.

She said, "I'll see you," and this time she made it out the door.

Jagger lay in quiet meditation on his bed. A prison guard escorted a newspaper reporter through the corridor, placed a chair on the floor, and turned it to face Jagger's cell.

"You should be good," the guard said to the reporter. "Any problems with him, just scream. I'll have my headphones on and I won't hear you, so scream really, really, really, really loud."

Sitting up now, watching her, Jagger didn't comment. He only stared at her.

The guard turned and walked off back down the corridor.

She took the seat in front of Jagger's cell.

"Hi, Jagger."

Jagger said, "LaVerne," in a soft tone, staring into the freckled face looking through the iron bars at him.

LaVerne said, "How did you know my name?"

Jagger let his gaze drop to her neck. "Your ID pass."

LaVerne said, "Oh, right." She released a nervous laughter. "For a second there, I thought you were my estranged stalker."

Jagger kept staring.

LaVerne, even more nervous under those uncanny eyes of this redheaded negro, said, "Okay, so far so good."

Her ID pass wasn't on her neck.

Jagger got up from his bed. He pulled an uncomfortable straight-back chair few feet to the cell bars, sat down and leaned forward on his arms, going along with the interview.

"I'm LaVerne Murphy, as you already know."

Silence.

It made her more nervous.

She said, "I'm a reporter for *The New York Times.*"

More silence.

"You read *The New York Times*?"

She stared back at Jagger and tried to wait him out.

He blinked. She startled.

"We don't read the paper in here," Jagger said. "Safety hazard, you see. The crazies in here like to eat the funny pages."

"Oh, I see. Well, I'd like to do an interview on you."

He already knew that.

"Do you have the time for an interview?"

"*Liefling*, time is all I have in here. So waste it away."

"What'd you call me?"

"Sweetheart."

LaVerne sighed deeply, affected by his soft-spoken accent, then brought her focus back to the interview. She said, "Okay, um, I'm writing a story on you, and I'd like to include your views."

He said, "If it's editing you want help with, I'm gonna tell you right now—we're both not very bright."

She didn't let herself get sidetracked by his humor. It was dry but cute.

Okay, we're sidetracking.

"Your parents moved from South Africa to New York, and after dropping off the map for twenty years, you showed up at their doorstep and butchered your mother." He made her so nervous. "I guess what I'm saying is—"

Jagger said, "You want tips." He paused and said, "I told myself, I should just write a book."

Millicent came at eleven.

Bobby said, "Why do doctors leave the room when you get changed? I mean they're gonna see you naked anyway, right?"

Millicent said, "I've been losing sleep on that too."

"You found a place yet?"

"As a matter of fact, I did. Oh, but then Nicki Minaj came and took it away."

Bobby raised his eyebrows. "No shit, Nicki Minaj got the condo you were after?"

"She didn't get the condo, her ghetto booty got her the condo. And the cutie real estate agent that came with it."

Millicent's cell phone rang.

She didn't move.

Bobby said, "You gonna answer?" She told him it was her bookie and it gave him a bad feeling. "Your bookie's calling you? That can't be good."

"He's been trying to get through to me. I don't have the time for him."

She rejected the call.

"Mill, you better make time," Bobby said. "You keep ducking your bookie's calls it's only gonna make him angry ... *er.*"

"What's my bookie gonna do?"

"The unimaginable. How'd he find out about you betting on yourself?"

"Last bitch I fought was so mad about the permanent scar I gave her that she tattled on me."

"*Millicent.*"

"I fucked up. But I'll take care of him."

"Pray he don't beat you to it and take care of you."

Her cell phone rang again with a scary sound.

Bobby stirred. "Oh, damn."

Millicent left and Matthew showed up at three with Danny. Matthew turned his head yelling to Danny, who was messing around in the lavatory, "Danny? I'm not going to tell you twice—come out of the bathroom!"

"Ah, let her play."

"She breaks anything in there, you're going to be replacing it."

Bobby shouted to her now, "Danny, for the love of God, come outta there!"

Matthew said, "You see where you are?"

Bobby frantically looked around. "Why, what? Where am I?"

"You think this is a joke, you sorry excuse for a brother?"

Bobby remembered Millicent and said, "Bro, I need to tell you something."

But Matthew was already saying, "You poison a man was your friend and you sit there and think it's funny?"

"Bro, believe me, you wanna hear this."

"What? What do I fucking want to hear?"

"Millicent's bookie found out she's betting on herself, and I think she may be in trouble."

It stopped Matthew's irritable mood and redirected him. "*What?*"

"I tell myself I ain't snitching—I just care too much."

They heard the toilet flush and Danny's voice:

"Uh-oh."

Matthew turned his overburdened mind toward the lavatory. "Why do I get the feeling that 'uh-oh' means it's too late?"

In the cell directly behind LaVerne lay a psychopathic prisoner, who was reclining on his bunk. This was Solomon, facing ten to fifteen for raping his aunt, Solomon lying on his back and staring at the ceiling, listening to the interview.

Listening to LaVerne say, "What is that?" to Jagger holding a dozen stones.

"They're my shaman stones," Jagger said. "They send me a reading on what's going on outside."

"Outside the prison? Does it work?"

"To those stupid enough to believe it, yes, it works wonders."

LaVerne said, "Jagger, do you recall what life was like for a child with cerebral palsy?"

"In my culture, a woman who gives birth to a disabled child is cursed."

"*Regtig?*"

Jagger picked up on it, that word in Afrikaans, and he said, "You're not from South Africa." He said, "Though you've been there. Once."

"I chased down a story a few years ago. It led me into a forest."

It intrigued him and he said, "Something else went down while you were in the forest." He wasn't asking, he was telling her he knew. Somehow he knew.

LaVerne bet he knew a lot more than he let on.

She moved the topic along saying, "So disabled children are cursed in Africa, huh?"

"I was seven, eight, so I don't remember much of it."

"What are the things do you remember?"

"There weren't enough food for us to eat. I starved a lot. A lot, a lot. The drought made it especially difficult for our family. We ate porridge once a day. Twice if God willed it."

"Wasn't there meat or bread or stuff like that?"

Jagger said, "You see, the way it works is, to eat the food you have to *buy* the food. It would've been easier if I'd been raised in Japan, 'least in Japan you eat right off a naked woman's body." He looked at her then. "You haven't quite recovered from your wanderings through the forest."

She cleared her throat and moved on. "Was that why your mother abandoned you in the forest? Because there was no food to feed the family?"

"My mother didn't leave me in the forest, my father did. But it was her idea, her plan. Had she taken me in the forest herself, she wouldn't have made it out. The forest is a dangerous place, especially for a woman. It would've come to life and skinned her alive. This you had discovered," Jagger said, looking at her. "Do you look back on it?"

LaVerne said, "I try not to."

Jagger heard a quiver in her voice.

"I can still smell him," LaVerne said. "He smelled of dirt and voodoo lilies."

"I'm very sorry," Jagger said. "Did they ever catch him?"

"No, he got away. I didn't get a look at him, although he did leave his mark on me. And it took six years to wash off."

"There's another world deep in those forests," Jagger said, "and it's a world nothing like what you see on the surface. Deep in these forests of Africa lives something evil. Something unimaginable. Something out of a nightmare, so much so that only fearless bush-meat hunters dare enter its deepest, darkest bowels and survive. And to be successful, hunters have to possess some mastery, without which they'd never again see home."

"Your father took you into this forest?"

"I remember being wrapped in a blanket," Jagger said, "and my father holding me close to him. It was a long journey. We stopped only once."

"Is that when he left you?"

"No, that's when my father started crying. He cried for a long time, and then he wiped his tears and went further into the forest. It was dark by then. I remember the feeling of the ground beneath me as he laid me under a tree." Jagger paused. "And then he left me there." He said, "You see, they rid themselves of the children who're unable to walk back home."

"Why did your parents choose to take you into the forest?"

Jagger waited. "So animals could eat me."

He'd bought the sports car for both of them to enjoy. If he'd known she'd hate it, he wouldn't have bothered. No, wait. That wasn't exactly true. It wasn't the sports car that frightened her. It was his driving. What was wrong with driving fast? Craig was born in a family of race car drivers. If you didn't drive fast, you weren't driving.

Tuesday afternoon, half past twelve, Craig took off from his house in his Porsche, full of rage. He stopped at the liquor store and bought Irish whiskey, a Black Bush for the road. He sped off, not caring where he went. As he drove aimlessly around town, he started drinking and chain-smoking. He became reckless, driving as fast as the Porsche would go. It was when his phone rang that another accident happened. He propped the bottle of Black Bush between his thighs and picked up his phone. He didn't see the kid in the double-layered T-shirts step off his skateboard and into the road. The Porsche bore down on him. Craig's subconscious mind screaming at him to *look where you're going, you Irish fool!* Craig's eyes came up and he saw the kid through the windshield, the kid crossing the road, the car hurdling toward him. Craig cranked the wheel and the Porsche ran off the road and crashed into a funeral home, the impact throwing him into a display of caskets.

He woke up and found himself lying in one.

A hand nudged his ribs and he looked up to see the undertaker looming over him. Craig sat up right away, winced from an excruciating pain that came from a place that was not locatable. He said, "Jesus Christ," seeing his beautiful Porsche half in and half out the window. The British undertaker asked if he was all right.

"Am I dead?"

"Well, if you aren't, you woke up in the nick of time."

The bookie sent his goons out after Millicent. They lurked in the crowd of people in the warehouse watching the fight.

"That's our girl in the red," the first goon said as he spotted Millicent in the maroon jersey vest, and the second goon answered, "We gotta make sure."

They retreated from the noisy crowd.

Outside in darkness, Matthew sat in the Jaguar, shrewdly watching the two goons come out of the warehouse and get into a black sedan.

Solomon was no longer staring at the ceiling. The psychopathic rapist was off his bunk and staring quietly through the bars of his cell at LaVerne's back.

Neither Jagger nor LaVerne noticed Solomon.

LaVerne asking Jagger, "Someone in the forest came for you?"

Locked behind bars, Jagger said, "Not someone ... something. I could hear the sound of a bell coming toward where I lay. It was the most charming sound. Its possessor drew closer ... And then I saw it. This creature the size of a dwarf with gouged out eyes and a snout that could open wide to devour a human being, be he alive or dead, a spirit of the forest with long, razor-sharp claws.

"I felt it. It lifted me off the ground and carried me away to its dwelling. Kept me for twenty years. It fed me and clothed me in leaves. Showed me things, taught me stuff."

LaVerne was staring at him. "This creature that came out of the woods and took you, what exactly was it?"

"Had it not come to take me, I could've died in those woods. Or worse, I could've been eaten by animals."

There was a weighty silence. LaVerne watched Jagger through the bars. She noticed how the lights from the prison yard shone through the small window and illuminated his abnormal red hair.

"Jagger?" She waited.

Jagger looked over and met her eyes.

"What was this creature that came and took you?"

"They were more than one, a whole hamlet of them. They raised me as their own. They became my family. I was their one and only link to the people living outside the forests, whom they lionized."

Did she hear him right, did he say ... LaVerne said, "They?"

"Tokoloshes."

"Tokoloshe?"

"Tokolo-*shes*—plural. That's what they're called." Jagger paused, looking off and smiling. Something was in the corridor with LaVerne. "You're gonna hear bells. When you do, don't move. You do, you'll die."

"What?"

Then came the ringing of said bells. He warned her not to move. LaVerne stiffened in her chair. Jagger said, "They want you to sit still." He was scaring her, he knew, but she had to remain absolutely still.

The chair she was sitting on rose off the floor by invisible forces. An inch. Two. Three inches. Four. LaVerne stiffened even more. Now she was a foot up, then two feet off the corridor floor. Then, slowly, LaVerne was lowered down again, and she saw the Tokoloshes. They stood child-like, three feet tall and hairy, two creatures, shades of red, one postured at each side of LaVerne's chair. She jumped to her feet and cried out in hysterics. "Oh my God, oh my God, oh my God, oh my God!"

Without caution she backed up too close to Solomon's cell, close enough for the now naked Solomon to reach through his bars, grab her, and drag her against the cell. LaVerne screamed at the top of her lungs.

"LaVerne—" Jagger sprung from his chair.

Millicent was returning to the motel after the fight. She rounded the corner to a stretch of sidewalk ahead, street lights lighting the way for her. Tires screeched to a halt and the black sedan pulled up in front of her, blocked her path toward the motel, her sanctuary.

The two goons climbed out of the sedan.

"Millicent Dallis-Price?"

She said, "Yeah?"

They started to advance on her … and Matthew emerged from around the corner, out of the darkness, to stand behind her in street light, tall and powerful.

Threatened by his enormity, the goons backed up, and without a word they hopped into their sedan, and hightailed it away.

Millicent watched them go, unsure what just happened.

Matthew's protective eyes were on her.

She sensed someone behind her now, could feel their heat at her back. Their presence stirred the hairs at the nape of her neck.

She wheeled around and saw nothing but shadows.

Solomon had a hold of LaVerne up against the bars of his cell.

LaVerne was screaming.

Solomon saying, "Don't be scared, sweet cheeks." One of Solomon's hands left LaVerne's shoulder and cupped her breast. "Very nice. Love the feel. Wouldn't mind doing you right here, right now."

He thrust his bare genitals forward. LaVerne screamed some more.

"Oh my God! He's got me! He's got me! He's got me!"

Jagger, out of his cell and in the corridor, said, "Back off, Solomon! Back off," and freed LaVerne from Solomon's sadistic embrace.

"Well, goddammit, give me *some*thing."

LaVerne darted away from them and cringed against the barred doors of Jagger's cell, breathing so fast and so loud that it sounded like sobbing. She had narrowly escaped rape.

Jagger yelled at Solomon, "Back into your skin!"

There was a silence, quiet and thick, and in it was the shuddering panic of LaVerne's breathing. Then it stopped. LaVerne realizing Jagger was in the corridor. Though in his cell, his physical body, remained in the chair.

He was in a deep state of astral mediation.

LaVerne's jaw came unhinged. "Oh—my—*God*."

She tore her green eyes from the body of the Redheaded Negro in the cell, to his astral soul in the corridor. It stood solid by Solomon's cell, bathed in a subdued glow of warm light, that she had mistaken it for a real being. Jagger's lifelike soul went back to his cell, stepping through the iron bars, and slipped into his body.

Jagger came out of meditation and raised his head of fire engine red hair, quick, to warn his Tokoloshe brothers.

"*Gaan!*"

The Tokoloshes obediently vanished into thin air, bells ringing.

Guards ran into the corridor without seeing them.

"What's going on here?" The first guard saw Solomon naked in his cell. "Jesus Christ. Solomon, put your clothes back on. You want to make us all lose our lunch?"

The second guard took LaVerne by the arm and stood her on her feet. "Are you all right? Are you *hurt*?"

The first guard faced Solomon's cell. "And the socks—nobody wants to see your hammer toes."

"Did he hurt you?" the second guard said, but LaVerne didn't hear him.

She was staring at Jagger.

Jagger stared calmly back at her.

When Ray heard about it he said, "Dude you crashed into a funeral home?"

"I swear to God, that funeral home came out of nowhere," Craig said. He now occupied the other bed in Bobby's hospital room.

"Did that kid come out of nowhere too?"

Bobby said to Craig, "Weren't you watching the road, man?"

"Not at first, no. By the time my mind was back on the road, my fate was sealed."

Ray gave him a concerned look. "But you're all right otherwise?

"Yeah, I'm all right. But you know, when I woke up in that casket . . . I thought I was a dead Irishman."

Bobby nodded. "That is a frightening thought."

"You guys were totally right," Craig said, "I drive like a madman. From now on I'm going to keep to the speed limit. And that is a promise." He thought about what he said and changed it to, "'Least till this whole incident blows over."

Ray said, "Ah, the parable of a madman."

ABOUT THE AUTHOR

I was born in 1987 in Ivory Coast, West Africa. At age two I fell ill and was taken to the hospital. There I was given an injection that paralyzed me. After many treatments by a witch doctor, I was able to regain my bodily functions but was affected by polio, and now I walk with a limp. My parents left me with my father's mother in Sekondi-Takoradi before coming to London in 1991. My father came back for me when I was four. I lived with them in St. Raphael's then moved to John Buck House on Fry Road. While there I attended New Field Primary School and studied English literature in Queens Park Community School and Harrow College. My parents divorced in 1996. In 1999, I developed depression due to my disability and went through numerous suicidal attempts. Ending my life was all I could think to do; it consumed me. My therapist advised me to put all my focus on something else. Though I possessed the gift of art, it didn't help. It was not a passion but more a trait. Then I discovered writing. First I started to write a diary, and then I went on to poetry and songs, until gradually I developed the feel for fictional writing. Fiction helped me forget my depression. I got addicted to writing, which gave me peace of mind and whisked me into a world that was not my own, and I absolutely loved it—that literary world that was unlike my reality. So I wrote morning, noon, and evening until I created a world of characters. I have written a group of nineteen novels, *Shepherd*, which I haven't published. I keep those for myself. After *Shepherd*, I moved with my mother and brother to Church Road, where my writing evolved. I'm currently composing a comedy-drama I call *Outside*, which has over 136 episodes, and there are more episodes that are in creation. Writing has made me antisocial. When I write, I get lost in my fiction and forget about the world around me. I forget about my suicide. My fiction is my rabbit hole where I escape from reality—it's my *Alice in Wonderland*.